Dreaming
In Color

Dreaming In Color

Ruth Moose

August House / *Little Rock*
P U B L I S H E R S

Published by August House, Inc.,
P.O. Box 3223, Little Rock, Arkansas 72203,
501-663-7300

Printed in the United States of America

10 9 8 7 6 5 4 3 2 1

LIBRARY OF CONGRESS CATALOGING-IN-PUBLICATION
DATA

Moose, Ruth.
Dreaming in color/Ruth Moose.—1st ed.
p. cm.
ISBN 0-87483-078-8 (alk. paper): $15.95
1. Women—Southern States—Fiction. I. Title.
88-7938
CIP
PS3563.069D74 1989
813'.54—dc19

First Edition, 1989

Cover illustration by Byron Taylor
Production artwork by Ira Hocut
Typography by Lettergraphics, Memphis, Tennessee
Design direction by Ted Parkhurst
Project direction by Hope Norman Coulter

This book is printed on archival-quality paper which meets the
guidelines for performance and durability of the Committee on
Production Guidelines for Book Longevity of the Council on
Library Resources.

The characters in this book are entirely fictitious.
Any similarities between them and actual persons
are coincidental.

AUGUST HOUSE, INC.   PUBLISHERS   LITTLE ROCK

Acknowledgments

"Daisy Wars" was first published as "The Marigold Wars and Therma Ann" in *Cardinal: An Anthology of North Carolina Writers*.

"Friends and Oranges" was first published in *New Delta Review*.

"The Green Car" was first published in *Crop Dust*.

"He Holds a Black Umbrella" was first published as "Jesus Christ and Other Salesmen" in *Ohio Review*.

"King of the Comics" first appeared in *Crucible*.

Contents

Peanut Dreams and the Blue-Eyed Jesus

WHEN SHELBY JEAN FOSTER first hears about the photograph of Jesus, she is twelve. She has long dark hair, thick bangs, and wide eyes. She has never known anyone like Ellis Nickerson in her life and she doesn't know what to think. She doesn't believe Ellis. Shelby hasn't believed a lot of what Ellis has told her, but this photograph stuff is the most unbelievable thing Ellis has said yet. Ellis says she has not only seen the photograph, but knows the girl who took the picture. Two weeks after the girl first took the picture, she died. Just like that. Ellis snaps her finger in the air.

Shelby Jean has been going to Sunday school all her life and she knows, if she doesn't know anything else, that Jesus died a long time before the camera was invented.

When Ellis sees that Shelby Jean doesn't believe her, she gets red, puffs out her cheeks, and acts huffy. That's the only word for it—huffy. Ellis says she can get the photograph and show Shelby. Then Shelby will have to believe her.

"If the girl who took the photograph is dead," Shelby Jean

says, "how are you going to get it?"

"She lives in Locust Lick." Ellis lights a cigarette, tilts her head, and blows smoke in a blue cloud toward the ceiling.

Shelby Jean really doubts the whole thing then. She never heard of Locust Lick until Ellis started talking about it. And when she tried to pin Ellis down about where Locust Lick was, Ellis would say quickly, "Down in the eastern part of the state."

"What's it close to?" Shelby would ask. "I mean what's the largest city?"

"Nothing," Ellis would say. "It's between nothing and close to nothing." Then she would laugh big, as if she'd made a joke. Shelby thought that was rude, but then that was Ellis.

Shelby tried to find Locust Lick on the North Carolina map, spreading counties and roads, rivers and cities across her desk, trailing some over onto her bed. Nothing. Locust Lick wasn't even a chigger-sized dot on the map in the eastern part of the state or anywhere else. It wasn't even in the index of cities.

When she told Ellis, Ellis snorted, "I'm not surprised. Half the county don't even know where Locust Lick is. Much less the state. They never heard of Raleigh down there. For your information"—she paused, looked Shelby Jean directly in the eyes—"Locust Lick is a little slow-down place in the middle of the road between Elizabethton and Warrenington. It's got five houses, a service station, and a post office. I should know. My daddy runs both."

Shelby didn't know whether to believe Ellis or not. Locust Lick, her daddy, and all. Ellis said every seven years people remembered Locust Lick because that was where they had the festival. The Locust Festival, she added when Shelby acted like she hadn't heard.

"That's when they have the locust races," Ellis said, "and eat fried locusts to see who can eat the most. Last festival a man ate six hundred. Fried! They have chocolate-covered locusts for dessert and locust beer," Ellis went on. "Then at midnight there's a street dance and fireworks. Don't tell me you never heard of it."

Shelby hadn't. She asked her mother who said Lord knows what people would do these days. And she had heard of a locust beer. It was made from pods off a locust tree she thought grew in North Carolina but she'd never seen one that she knew.

Shelby still doesn't know whether to believe the Locust Festival, Locust Lick, and all. She doesn't know how much of Ellis to believe. It seems Ellis appeared out of nowhere. One day late in August, she and Truett Deal moved into the Hyatts' garage apartment. "It didn't look like they had six sticks of furniture," Mrs. Hyatt told Shelby's mother. "Kids. Both of them. I got my rent in advance though so I won't be out. If they move tomorrow, I won't be out anything."

The next day Ellis Nickerson, she never called herself Ellis Deal, which made Shelby's mother and Mrs. Hyatt glance at each other, knocked on the Fosters' front door. She asked if she could use their phone, then started using it twice, three and sometimes five times a day. Shelby's mother didn't mind the first few times. They were new in the neighborhood, a young couple and all. After a while she said she didn't see why Ellis came to their house, it was Hyatts she rented from. If anybody should bend over backwards to be nice to Ellis and True, it should be the Hyatts. But she never says this to Ellis, who most of the time doesn't even call back a thank-you when she finishes with the phone, just leaves and slams the door.

When Ellis comes to use the phone she is usually calling Truett, True as she always calls him, to bring her a popsicle or sack of potato chips or mostly just to ask how much longer it will be before he comes home. He never gets home before dark. It is as if Ellis thinks by calling him she can get him to hurry or change things. But he doesn't.

Shelby's mother says that if she keeps it up, she will make

Truett lose his job. That George Arnold doesn't pay people to stand around his service station and talk on the phone.

In the weeks before school starts, sometimes Ellis and Shelby Jean walk to town. The town has a few old-fashioned stores that have not yet moved to the shiny new mall out on the bypass. Shelby likes to get her school supplies early. She can spend an hour choosing a notebook, clicking the rings, testing the backs of the binders. She likes to see her school supplies laid out neatly and newly bright on her desk in her bedroom. Ellis says, "You aren't going to find out what life's all about in a book, sitting in some dumb room copying words off a blackboard." She says she spent more time riding school busses than she ever did in a classroom. That's where you learn things. Who is going with who. Who did what after the last football game. Who is going after who with a shotgun. "You don't need to know anything to be married," she tells Shelby Jean with a wide smile, "except the most important thing."

"What's that?" Shelby asks.

But Ellis only licks her lips and says, "If you have to ask, you don't need to know."

Shelby knows. Her mother gave her a book with diagrams and little drawings and pictures. She has seen the film at school. The whole thing doesn't seem like such a big deal. She thinks of married people as old. Like her parents. Like the Hyatts. Like everybody in the neighborhood, except Ellis who is too smart for her own good, Shelby's mother says. In every way but where she needs to be. "It will catch up with her," Mrs. Foster says. "Wait and see."

Every Sunday Ellis and Truett sleep late. Sometimes they never leave their apartment at all. The door stays closed, shades pulled all day, even though Mrs. Foster, Mrs. Hyatt, and others in the neighborhood have invited them again and again to the red brick Methodist church on the corner.

Shelby has gone to the church forever, it seems. Sometimes she stands under the lighted picture of Jesus in the basement hall that smells of cement and paint. She studies the picture. The kind blue eyes, thick brown hair, very dark beard. She thinks of Jesus as very good-looking. Her father, most of the men she knows and sees every day, are very plain, or bald, wear glasses. Jesus looks healthy, like he has a year-round tan. She thinks it is from being outside with all those sheep. The picture is cardboard, loose from its frame. When some of the older boys go by, they take a swipe at the picture, send it askew. Shelby always waits for lightning to strike them immediately or at least a hailstorm outside when they get there. Ice balls pelting their head and them crying help, help. But nothing happens. She straightens the picture and wants to feel some good blessing fall around her shoulders.

When Shelby describes the picture to Ellis, Ellis says it sounds like the ones you can buy everywhere and a church as rich and fancy as the one on the corner ought to have something better. She's seen those Jesus pictures at the dimestore. Ellis spends a lot of time in the dimestore in town. She goes maybe two or three times a week. She walks to town just to look. Most of the time she doesn't buy anything but a cherry Coke and some Nabs, sits in the drugstore booth and sucks ice. "They got the prettiest towels in Rose's," she tells Shelby. "Yellow leaves. They'd look so good when we get our house." She slides a plastic ring from the bubble-gum machine back and forth on her finger. Truett was going to buy her a wedding band, she says, but she didn't want one of those plain old things like her mother had. She wants a real diamond. A big one. And until then she doesn't want one at all.

In the few days before school opens, Shelby Jean walks with Ellis to town. Ellis wears cut-off jeans, a tank top T-shirt, and flat, floppy sandals. Beside her Shelby's wearing pink shorts and a frilly white blouse and bounces when she walks. She feels like an ice cream cone. Strawberry. Shelby's hair is pulled back and tied with a pink ribbon so it flips and sways. Truck drivers hoot their horns, whistle and wave. Ellis waves and whistles back, acts like she is going to run after them. When one slows and opens his door, Ellis grabs Shelby's arm and acts like she wants to run and hide behind the nearest bush.

Ellis is pregnant now. Even though she keeps saying it, Shelby Jean doesn't know whether to believe her or not. Her stomach doesn't seem to be getting any bigger. Not in one spot. She's gaining weight all over; face, arms, hands, feet, especially her breasts. Ellis says she has grown two cup sizes in two months. Shelby Jean is still in a training bra. Ellis shows Shelby some of her black lace bras, pink satin ones, flesh-colored ones. When Shelby's mother sees them on her clothesline she says they are the tackiest things and she hopes for goodness sakes no one thinks they belong to anyone in *her* family. She looks at Shelby when she says this, as though Shelby is tainted being around Ellis. Mrs. Foster knows Shelby owns no underwear that is not the whitest of white. It is Mrs. Foster who lets Ellis use their clothesline after she goes to the coin washerette on the corner. Ellis pushes their laundry in a shopping cart that squeaks in all four wheels. Mrs. Foster thinks it was probably stolen, but Ellis swears True says someone left it at the station. Most of the time Shelby's mother has her own wash dried and folded and put away before Ellis gets around to hanging hers out. Then at eleven o'clock at night, Shelby sees Truett like a ghost in their back yard gathering in laundry. He always whistles some Willie Nelson tune that Shelby can hear long after he leaves.

Ellis sleeps late, then watches her "programs"—soap operas that make Shelby's mother shake her head and say, "All that will change once the baby gets here." And, "Then she'll see what she got herself into." She sighs, but Shelby hears the warning aimed at her. It has hit its mark. Shelby does not plan to let her life go in the same direction Ellis has taken, but something about Ellis interests her. Ellis seems so much older than anyone she knows, but not old in the same way as her mother or Mrs. Hyatt.

Now that Shelby is in junior high she rarely sees Ellis. Shelby is caught up in school. She is trying out for cheerleader and stays after school to practice. She can do the yells and the motions that go with them, but she never kicks quite high enough. And she absolutely cannot do the split. Her mother doesn't like to see Shelby trying to do the split in the back yard. She says girls can damage themselves. They spend the rest of their lives paying for it. Shelby doesn't care if she can only be selected cheerleader. The white wool skirts are so short and cute. The red vests with the big letter *A* on them. And the red pom-poms. Shelby can see one hanging in her room above the mirror on her dresser with her dance card from the Spring Fling. She was one of the few fourteen-year-olds invited, but she is not chosen cheerleader and cries herself to sleep for several nights. Her mother buys her a new plaid skirt and yellow sweater, leather loafers, button bag.

On Shelby's nightstand is a plastic cross that glows in the dark. Mrs. Frome, her Sunday school teacher, gave every girl a cross last year for Christmas. Sometimes Shelby wakes in the night and her cross is not glowing. She wants to ask the other girls if theirs work all night, but she is afraid Mrs. Frome will overhear and be hurt. Once in a while, the thing Ellis said about the photograph of Jesus crosses Shelby's mind. She knows it is something Ellis made up because Ellis has not mentioned it since. Nor Locust Lick. Ellis was trying to impress Shelby and now that she has seen she doesn't have to, she has stopped, settled down.

One day after school, Ellis is sitting on the bottom step of their garage apartment. She invites Shelby in for a Coke and to see her new maternity clothes. Ellis has jeans with a hole cut in the stomach, a dotted blouse with little tucks and smocked yoke. She shows Shelby her baby bottle filled with pink and blue capsules she takes every day. Each time she gets her prescription filled, she gets another bottle. By the time the baby comes, she will have enough. The way she says it, by the time the baby comes or *when* the baby comes, Shelby feels like glancing at the door, as though the baby is expected like any guest to step through it.

It is Christmas vacation before Shelby sees Ellis again. She taps at the door and Ellis, in the same quilted robe full of burn spots, pulled threads, and dangling buttons, answers it. There are greasy dishes in the sink and the whole apartment has a sour smell. Shelby doesn't stay, but when Ellis says she has a doctor's appointment the next afternoon and Shelby has to go to the library to research a paper on the American Revolution, they decide to go together.

Shelby feels as if she ought to get Ellis a Christmas present, but she doesn't know what. The little green bush of a tree Ellis has in the middle of her table is so sad. Ellis tried to decorate it with a dozen red and blue balls, a few strands of icicles. There is one present under it.

"I know," Shelby tells Ellis. "Why don't you get your ears pierced? That will be my present to you for Christmas. And you get a set of earrings when they pierce them."

Ellis looks excited. She likes the idea. They stand in line at Belk's, and Ellis signs the release form. They select earrings. Ellis doesn't like the tiny gold button ones, but wants earrings that dangle. Shelby tells her you have to start out with the plain ones. Shelby and Ellis lean over the glass counter looking at all the earrings while they wait. The smell of alcohol is strong. When the nurse punches holes in the ears of the little girl in front of them, she lets out a scream you can hear all over the store. Tears roll down her face and wet her dress. "That didn't hurt," her mother says.

"Yes, it did," the little girl screams. "It still hurts." She holds her ears. The mother pulls her from the store, still screaming. Only one ear pierced.

Ellis steps from the line. Shelby Jean follows. "Aren't you going—?"

PEANUT DREAMS AND THE BLUE-EYED JESUS

"I've changed my mind," Ellis says. "I didn't like any of those earrings anyway."

They buy popcorn from Rose's and share the bag all the way home. The popcorn is warm and fresh. Even the butter flavoring doesn't taste stale. "I bet I've gained ten pounds," Ellis giggles. "True says he doesn't care if I get big as a house. He loves me just the same."

In January, Shelby is at the drugstore. This is where all the kids from school stop first thing. There is no music, but no one could hear it if there was. Everyone screams. You can't hear yourself think. Shelby and some of the seniors she knows get a booth together. They like the tables better because the booths are old and have splinters and sometimes pick their pantyhose. She sees Ellis at the prescription counter. Ellis is wearing a bulky green coat and looks big as a truck. Her hair is oily and limp, her face blotched. The dotted top is hiked in front and wrinkled. Shelby hopes Ellis won't see her, but she does. She stops at Shelby's booth, stands with her packages and purse against her protruding stomach. She says hello, looks at Shelby with a weak little smile.

Shelby thinks Ellis looks as old as her mother or Mrs. Hyatt, yet she knows she is the same age as Leigh beside her. Or Ann across the table. Not yet seventeen. Shelby sips her Coke, stirs her ice with the straw, stares at the tabletop. The room is a field of books, letter jackets, cheerleading costumes, so noisy. She doesn't know what to say, so she mumbles something about the crowd. Her friends stare at her, their eyes amused, asking how do you know this person? Who is she? Ellis smiles and waits. She brushes her hair back and Shelby sees her nails are chipped. Ellis used to spend hours on her nails until they looked like pictures in magazines. She isn't wearing any lipstick. Ellis shifts her packages. She stands on one foot, then shifts her weight and bulk to the other.

Shelby feels hot. Her mouth is dry and all her friends are

waiting for her to say something. Ellis drops her smile into a look that hits the floor like something Shelby can hear. Her eyes get dull and hurt. She turns and waddles through the crowd.

Shelby watches her back until it is out the door and down the street. Out of sight. She can still feel the pain in Ellis's face, the asking. Almost the *please* in her voice and eyes. Why didn't Shelby invite her to sit down? She should have asked. She should have introduced Ellis to everyone. She could have done that. It wouldn't have hurt . . . but what would her friends have thought? And Ellis was probably too big to get in the booth anyway. Still Shelby knows if she doesn't do something, she will feel that hurt. So she grabs her books, the rest of her Coke, and hurries out.

When she catches up with Ellis, neither of them says anything. They walk two blocks in the wind and silence. After a while Ellis rummages in her packages and opens a clear plastic purse full of chocolate candies. Peanut Dreams. From the drugstore? Shelby's favorite. Ellis eats one, crunching the peanuts loudly. Then she eats two more. Three. Finally she hands one to Shelby, who tries to refuse. Ellis forces it into Shelby's hand. The candy is sticky, lumpy with nuts, whitish on top. It looks stale and possibly wormy. It smells like mothballs and the oil Rose's uses to sweep their floors. And cardboard boxes. Shelby never eats anything from the Rose's counter. Those open glass bins. You don't know who has had their hands in there, her mother says. Or where their hands have been. Shelby doesn't want to hurt Ellis's feelings. "Eat it," Ellis says.

But Shelby cannot.

Ellis eats the rest of the way home, pushing crumpled red papers from each piece back into the plastic purse as she empties them. "Probably make my face worse," she says, her voice flat and tired. "I'm already retaining fluid."

Shelby's candy has melted in her hand, stuck her fingers together. If it were forced down her throat she would immediately throw it up. That would hurt Ellis more. She slides it into the deepest corner of her coat pocket where she hopes it won't stain through. At least not until she gets home.

Ellis doesn't talk about the baby today. Nor True. She used to tell Shelby being married was the sweetest thing in the world. Today she doesn't talk much at all.

In March when Ellis has her baby, Shelby hears her mother and Mrs. Hyatt talking. A little boy. Not little really. It weighs almost ten pounds. And Ellis didn't have the easy time of it she thought she was going to have. "You never do," Shelby's mother says and Mrs. Hyatt quickly adds, "Amen to that." They have bought receiving blankets for the baby. They take their gifts to Ellis along with a meatloaf and casserole of scalloped potatoes. When they come back they talk about what a mess the apartment is. Newspapers and dirty clothes everywhere. Everywhere. Mrs. Hyatt says she is glad she didn't see the bathroom. The sight of that kitchen was enough. They talk about calling Ellis's parents—or the county health department.

Shelby doesn't know who they call and she doesn't know what she can do. She wants to see the baby. She has even bought a pair of white felt beaded moccasins for it. They have been in a clear plastic case on her dresser for several weeks now.

When she gets home from school the next day, there is a rusty red pickup truck parked in front of Ellis's garage apartment. It has wooden rails on the sides and something about "Farm and Home Supply" painted on the doors. Then below it, "Locust Lick, N.C." So there really is such a place, Shelby thinks as she changes from jeans to a wool jumper she wore a lot last year. It is so tight she can hardly get it zipped, but it looks dressier than jeans. She wraps the moccasins in white tissue and puts a blue bow on top. At Ellis's door, she knocks so timidly she has to knock again. A large woman in a sweatshirt and black polyester slacks opens it. She is wearing an apron and wipes her hands as she invites Shelby in. Shelby sees a man in a hat in the brown chair Ellis usually sits in to watch her soaps. The man is watching a game show on television or asleep. He doesn't turn around or speak. The woman says she is Ellis's mother and takes Shelby to the bedroom.

Ellis is in a gown in bed. There is a wicker basinette beside her and she gets up when she sees Shelby, smiles and takes the present. "Look at my big boy," she says, "while I open this."

Ellis holds the little shoes up and laughs, then unwraps the baby's foot from the blanket and compares them. The shoes that looked little on Shelby's dresser now look huge. They laugh and Ellis covers the baby back up. It is red and wrinkled. Shelby doesn't know what to say. "Isn't he beautiful?" Ellis says. "My big old boy."

She gets back in bed, arranges her pillows. "Don't ever have a baby," she says. "They do awful things to you. It wasn't having the baby that was so bad. It was the stuff they did to you first."

Ellis has a new robe, but Shelby sees one burn spot on the front already and her hair looks tangled and wild. Her eyes dart back and forth like minnows in a jar.

Shelby doesn't know what to do. She doesn't want to be in this room alone with Ellis. She has never seen Ellis like this, and when Ellis's mother comes in to ask if she would like a cup of coffee, Shelby is relieved. She says she really has to go and Ellis's mother says she understands. That Ellis doesn't need to wear herself out, but she is glad she has met some of Ellis's friends.

Some? Shelby thinks on the way home. There was nobody else. And she didn't really think of herself as a friend to Ellis. She was just someone who lived in the neighborhood closer to her age than her mother or Mrs. Hyatt. She and Ellis never did any fun things friends do. Not movies and football games, pajama parties, the drugstore—not any of those things.

After church on Sunday, Shelby has helped her mother with the dishes and started a report on the French and Indian War when her brother tells her someone is at the door to see her. She can't imagine who.

It is blustery cold, but Ellis and her mother are on the porch with the baby wrapped in a thick blue blanket. You can't even see his eyes nor face but the blanket wiggles so Shelby knows the baby is in there somewhere.

"I told Mama when she came to bring the photograph," Ellis says, "and she did."

For a minute Shelby thinks Ellis means a photograph of the baby. When Ellis hands the photograph to her, she can't understand it. The photograph is old. One of the corners is bent, another missing. All Shelby sees is black and white shapes, like a puzzle or shadow. "The photograph of Jesus. I told you about it," Ellis says, "the one the girl who lived in Locust Lick took."

"Oh." Shelby remembers, but she still can't see anything in the photograph.

"Right there." Ellie points. "See the beard. And hair. And his robe." All Shelby can see are two dots someone has made with a ballpoint pen.

"Eyes," Ellis says.

Shelby squints. For a moment she thinks she can see a figure in white with arms outstretched and a beard. But she isn't sure. It's just shapes. She hands it back to Ellis.

"I told you Mama would bring it," Ellis says, then adds that she is going home for a while.

"Till she gets straightened out," her mother says.

In the red truck someone honks the horn and they yell they are coming. To keep his shirt on. Ellis grinds out a cigarette on the Fosters' freshly painted porch. Shelby knows it will leave a scorch mark and her mother will say good riddance to bad rubbish.

Shelby tells Ellis goodbye. Then calls after Ellis, "I'll see you when you get back. Maybe it won't be so cold. Brrr." She wraps her arms around herself and shivers, runs back into the house.

For the next few weeks there are lights in the bedroom of the apartment, then none at all. True has moved out. Left. Gone. Just like that.

"Where did he go?" Shelby's mother asks Mrs. Hyatt.

"Who knows?" Mrs. Hyatt shrugs. "All I know is, he didn't leave owing me rent. If there's one thing I've learned all these years, it's get your money in advance."

One night as Shelby is almost asleep she remembers the photograph. That the girl who took it died two weeks later. She wonders if because she looked at it, she will die. Every night, she puts on a fresh nightgown and sleeps on her back so her hair will not be mussed. She gets a crick in her neck and makes a failing grade on a math test. Jimmy Reese invites her to his party. Nothing else happens.

The Women's Club

THEY WANT TO do away with October . . . it's convention month and nobody is at the meeting anyway. And January. Do away with it too. January comes so soon after Christmas. Everybody agrees. Their voices seem to say the nerve of that January coming so soon after Christmas whether it's wanted or not. January will be done away with unless someone speaks up. Anyone opposed?

No one is really opposed, but one member in a navy suit with white blouse of long frilly lace at neck and wrists waves her thin many-diamonded old hand. "January is Lee and Jackson month, Madam President, and I don't think we can do away with them."

Madam President says no one said anything about doing away with Jackson and Lee, just moving them to another month.

"State won't like it," another member mumbles.

"I don't care what State likes and doesn't like," says Madam President, her nose slightly wrinkled, pencil poised.

She seems about to strike the papers on the table beneath. "State isn't the one who has to do everything. Everything! Is there more discussion?" Her pencil checks out the room.

"What about June?" Another member leans forward on her cane. "That's always been Jefferson Davis month and I don't think we can change that without State saying something."

"Nobody," says Madam President Lucille Eppworth, "*nobody* said a word about doing away with June. If you'd just listen . . . just listen before you speak, you'd know which months are being done away with." As president of the chapter, Lucille wears a red, white, and blue ribbon pinned to her left breast. It dangles to her waist, gleaming with ten gold stars that dance in the candlelight. Candles for the Installation service.

"Anyone opposed?" Lucille says again. "Now's the time to speak up if you are. Not next week. Not next year. Not when it's your turn to hostess and you've got the month we tried to do away with. Speak up now so you won't grumble later."

No one opposes and the motion carries. Savannah Beauknight, the youngest member in both club years and age, sits in the last seat in the last row. Lucille bangs the gavel when she announces with vigor and a little smile that the motion carried. Savannah expects to see Lucille gather something in her arms (the motion?) and set it properly down. But she doesn't. Lucille goes on to the awarding of scholarships. The first one goes to her own "dear niece and namesake, a darling girl talented in every way and smart to boot." Lucille beams as she calls the girl forward.

"Just like her aunt." Lucille's vice-president, Jolene Hunsucker, smiles at the table. Jolene is cool in green linen and pearls.

The niece, Drucilla, goes forward. She's seventeen and fresh as a rose. Pert and pink and yes, even bright-looking, Savannah thinks. Drucilla wears a hat that matches her

dress, the only hat in the room. Odd, Savannah thinks, because most of these women have worn hats on most occa-
sions most of their lives. She mentally puts hats on them,
feathered red ones, white sailor straws, wide brims with
fruit and flowers and ribbon trims. She can't think why she
is at this meeting. Yes, she can. Because she still reacts to
Lucille Eppworth as she did when she was in the sixth grade
and bit her nails. Miss Eppworth was school principal, who
did things like nail examinations and behind-the-ear checks.
You never knew when she'd come to your classroom. Savannah remembers wanting to sit on her pink and stubby fingers to hide them from Miss Eppworth's eyes.

When Savannah and Charles moved back to Elliston, Lucille called. "We need you, dear," she said. "So many of our
members have passed." Passed? Savannah thought of grades
first, then realized with a little shock that wasn't what Lucille meant at all.

"We don't seem to be getting any new members," Lucille
went on. "Young women today stay too busy for their own
good and don't feel their obligations and responsibilities to
their communities like they should."

Guilt. Lucille ladled it out. "Your grandmother was one of
our dearest members and though your mother never joined
us, we so hope you will."

Savannah joined, was installed, pinned, hugged until she
felt she reeked of Estee Lauder in all twenty-eight flavors.

"Energy," Lucille said. "We need some of that energy to
help us out."

So far Savannah hadn't seen they needed anything but her
dues. She'd been in line at the A&P when Lucille ap-
proached her from Produce, a honeydew like a newborn in
her arms. "Sweetie, I know you've forgotten . . . it's so easy
to let time slip right past . . . your dues come up this month.
If you'll give me yours right now, I'll see Irene gets them on
time and you won't be a minute late."

Savannah planned to drop out. She'd been to one meeting

all year. The meeting where they showed slides of the Grand Canyon one of the members had taken from a mule. Everything tilted and blurred. But Lucille blocked the aisle at the A&P with her hand out, purse open. Savannah wrote her check for dues.

They made her Chaplain when she missed the next meeting. "Your grandmother could pray the sweetest prayers ever heard," Lucille said, "and I know you learned at her knee."

Lord, thought Savannah, get me out of this. "I'm really not very good . . ."

"Of course you are, darling," Lucille said. "And we'll all help you. It's a wonderful way to start. We need you so much."

At the next meeting (the time was ungodly—Friday afternoons at three o'clock), Savannah led the Collect. It was printed on little cards with Chaplain in italics, then Response in bold. They all pledged three times. The United States flag, the state flag, and finally the Confederate flag, "in remembrance." And because they didn't know if Savannah would be present, Randleman Sipes had written a prayer just in case. Savannah was relieved. Off the hook for another month.

Then she honestly forgot the next meeting. She bumped into Zillah Mayfield at the post office, who clasped her forearm and said steelily, "We *missed* you at the meeting."

"Meeting?" Savannah couldn't think what meeting.

"The chapter, of course, darling," Mrs. Mayfield said. "You're our Chaplain, you know. And when you don't come, someone else has to take charge."

Six people pushed around Savannah, still held in the iron grip of Mrs. Mayfield. "I forgot," she said.

"Forgot?" Mrs. Mayfield said. "Forgot!" Blue tears gathered in the corner of each pale eye. "Oh, my dear, we mustn't ever do that."

She let go as Savannah pulled toward the door. "Promise to try to do better next month, dear." Mrs. Mayfield's silver curls ringed her head, each sculpted and individual. Light shone through them in a halo effect.

Savannah would have forgotten again, had a member not called to remind her. "May we expect you tomorrow?"

Savannah gulped, "I don't know if . . ."

"It's our covered dish and last meeting of the year. We install new officers and I want our attendance to be good."

She'd said the two magic words. *Last meeting.* Savannah said yes and forgot again until noon. No time to make anything, she really had a good excuse this time, but she kept thinking last meeting, last meeting, so she quickly put together a Three Ps Casserole, dropped on some grated cheese, ran it under the broiler and shoved it into a silver dish, then dashed out the door. Somehow she had a feeling the food didn't count as much as the container.

There were a dozen cars in the parking lot. Last meeting, Savannah remembered. One car's motor idled with the doors locked and no one in the driver's seat. Savannah tried to turn the ignition off, but couldn't get in. She asked in the kitchen, but no one seemed to know whose car it was until Lucille bustled toward the meeting room. "That's Lauraellen's car. She does that all the time. It's a wonder that car hasn't run off and left her, or tried to. Give me the keys." She went to a woman in red silk. "Let me go see to it."

They formed a serving line, pushed Savannah in front. "You go first. You come so seldom, you're like a guest," Lucille chirped.

Savannah took a corner table and placemat of a white-columned azalea-blooming plantation. She was joined by her high school music teacher, who hadn't seemed to age as much as grow smaller and speak slower, more precisely. "You know I wrecked my car," Mrs. Priester says.

"No." Lauraellen Mayfield leans across the table. "I bet you went to sleep at the wheel."

"How did you know?" Mrs. Priester bends her head, ashamed.

"Because that's what I always do," Lauraellen says with a jerk of her chin. "Last time I just steered right off the road and even in my sleep I turned that curve as pretty as you please."

"In your sleep?" Mrs. Priester raises an eyebrow. "Really?"

"If I hadn't, I would have gone right into a tree. I was sound asleep, but I knew to turn that wheel." Lauraellen turns an imaginary wheel in the air. "And there was Harold sitting right beside me all the time reading the map. He didn't know we'd gone off the road until we stopped."

"What did you do then?" Savannah asks. She has taken a mound of chicken salad onto her plate. It looks like wallpaper paste. It tastes like wallpaper paste. She can't possibly eat it.

Lauraellen stops her fork and stares at Savannah. "Why honey, this was in Florida. I just drove right back up on that road like I'd never been off and nobody knew the difference."

"Oh." Savannah can't think what else to say. She has swallowed the mouthful of chicken salad.

"I had three people with me," Mrs. Priester says.

"And nobody said a word," Mrs. Priester repeats. "Until we all got out and looked at what I'd done."

"Oh," Savannah says again, drinking tea to wash down the wallpaper paste that is stuck in her throat. Tea so thick with sugar it coats her tongue. She waves away offers of dessert. Pound cake. Miss Ann made it. Her mama's recipe. "We can always depend on our Miss Ann for dessert," Lucille says loudly and everyone laughs. Miss Ann is also a music teacher. She loves to emphasize that she teaches privately and has her own studio downtown. "I could never use my home," she said once to Savannah. "That wouldn't do at all. You simply have no privacy, and privacy is one of the basic needs."

Miss Ann is nearly seventy, lives alone in a house that looks down over the town and can't be seen except in winter for the high unpruned magnolia trees around it. Trees and a tall wrought-iron fence. Miss Ann wears white cotton socks with sandals and a blue bow in her hair. She blushes as pink as her scalp when Lucille says she has never tasted a pound cake as good as Miss Ann makes.

When the dishes are returned to the kitchen (they never use paper plates; never have, never will), Savannah puts chairs back in rows, folds up a table, the only one left standing—hers. Somehow everything has been whisked back into place in the blink of an eye. Savannah slides the table toward the hall closet where others are stored behind louvered doors. "Darling, you are so sweet to help." Lucille flies past taking off her organdy apron as she goes. "But that's the table we *always* leave out for the guest registry. Leave it there for now, that's all right . . . for now."

Savannah puts the table up again and by the double front doors underneath the shiny photograph of Miss Agnes Overmyer. Miss Agnes passed last year at ninety-eight. She had been the one to donate land for building the woman's club. "We needed a little place to ourselves," she said, "for little meetings, parties and bridge."

"But we paid for the building," Lucille has always been quick to point out. "Every cent, every dollar, and it wasn't easy."

"How?" Savannah asks.

"Why, honey, don't you know? Every way we could. That's how you do things. You have bridge benefits and bake sales and more bake sales until before you know it, the thing's paid for." Lucille's eyes don't stop moving the whole time she talks. Nor her hands. She's like a hummingbird.

The officers of the woman's club are installed by Mrs. Priester, whose musical voice Savannah remembers rolling along in folksongs over and over, silver pitchpipe sounding the first twangy note. As each officer is called, Lucille serving as Madam President again, the green linen lady vice-president, Lauraellen Mayfield secretary—again. And Irene

Hautman, treasurer—again. They go through program chairman and corresponding secretary until every member is standing at the front of the room being installed. Only Savannah sits in the audience. She *is* the audience. She wants to laugh, but it is like the chicken salad, stuck in her throat. Instead she coughs. The ladies blink. It is as if she has taken their photograph. This is the moment later. They move from the ranks and back to their lives. Savannah takes the photograph home and for a long time finds it hard to flip past the images lodged like a slide caught crosswise in a projector, light cutting off the corners and edges until the whole thing rounds like an eye. The projector fan hums in her head and the dust motes of all time dance, dance like things alive in the air.

The Girl Who Looked Like Irma Budd's Little Sister

THE WOMAN IN the red coat with fur collar, wind whipping her waxy cheeks, walked through the three o'clock throngs of children knotted in front of Fairview Elementary. At the corner, she turned on her heels like a sentry, walked back again. Ted Hartman, the bus driver, Ronnie Apple, the cop at the crossing, the kids, some with books balanced on their heads, others playing keep-away with a purple toboggan, acted as if they didn't see her. The woman walked as invisibly through them as a spirit, untouched by their scuffling, yelling, and screaming. At the opposite corner she wheeled, walked through the crowd again.

Across the street, Mary Emmett Spratt stood on a stool by her bay window. "That wind won't do Rosalie Ritchie—"

"—any good," said Loveda, Mary Em's sister. Lov sat at the table cracking pecans. A gray wool plaid skirt covered her legs in folds to the floor where toes of her embroidered black slippers peeked out like kittens.

"Especially not in—" Mary Em glanced out the window.

"—her condition." Lov squeezed the silver jaws of the nutcracker until the pecan exploded, popped hulls that landed like insects on Mary Em's red braided rug.

"I wish you wouldn't do that." Mary Em studied the part in Lov's gray hair, the woven figure-eight braids across the back of her neck.

Lov wrinkled her forehead like a paper fan. "It's the only way I know to get the meat out."

Mary Em meant she wished Loveda wouldn't always finish her sentences for her. It got tiresome. A person had a right to finish something she started, her own thoughts even. It's still my house, she wanted to say a dozen times a day. Lov had retired from her Civil Service job in Washington six months before and moved in with Mary Em. There was no reason she shouldn't—with Hilbert dead and Mary Em rattling around in that big old house. No reason at all.

"Every day"—Mary Em taped another Christmas card to the red streamer attached to the cornice—"rain, shine, snow—Rosalie's out there, back and forth in front of that school." Lov's cards covered the left half of the streamer. Cards from people Mary Em didn't know. Cards with strange names that made Lov coo and give her silly laugh. "People cut down their mailing this year," Mary Em said. Her end of the streamer was a few cards scattered as patchwork. It looked skimpy even after she put up some cards from last year. If Lov had so many friends, why didn't she go live with them?

"I feel so sorry for her." Lov shifted the basket in her lap. Pecans piled high, like little brown eggs a wooden bird might have laid. "Rosalie Ritchie is young to have been through so much. Losing first that boy and now this one."

"What do you mean, this one?" Mary Em watched the tiny treadmill figure of the red-coated Rosalie. "She ain't had it yet."

"But it's dead." Lov threw a shriveled nutmeat into the trash. "The doctors say there's no chance it's still alive. And she won't give it up. Won't let her baby be taken."

"When did you find this out?" Mary Em pressed her nose to the cold glass that frosted so quickly she couldn't see anything but a blur of colored dots where the children stood, a smear of cars, black fumes of bus exhaust, and the wavering figure of Rosalie, walking, walking. "She looks like—"

"—Irma Budd's little sister," Lov said. "I've thought so too for a long time. There's something about her—the way she holds her head, that dark hair . . ."

Irma Budd had been Mary Em's best friend in high school, killed in a car accident the night of the spring cotillion. Her little sister had a nervous breakdown afterward, was "sent off."

"Whatever happened to—?" Lov lifted out the perfect pecan half, held it with long, tong-like fingers.

"Darlene Budd? I don't remember." Lov had such long fingers and Papa spent a fortune on piano lessons for her. What did she do with them? Once in a while Mary Em heard her out in the cold, dark old music room picking out one-finger tunes. Recital pieces children played. It helped her typing, Mama used to say, and that got her that good job. Manual dexterity. "If you're going to do that"—Mary Em wiped the frosted window with her sleeve—"be careful of your nails. I read in the paper you could sell them for so much a quarter-inch."

"I got a fortune then." Lov held her hands to the light, spread her fingers, white nails shining like candle flames.

"When did you hear about Rosalie Ritchie's baby being dead?" Mary Em shuddered. She couldn't imagine carrying a dead thing around inside you. How awful.

"Somebody who lives next door to the Ritchies told it at Circle last week."

"I didn't hear it and I—"

"—keep up," Lov said. "Yes, I know you do."

"I must have been out of the room." Mary Em put away the stool she'd stood on. "I sure didn't hear anything said about Rosalie Ritchie." Several cars clogged the crosswalk and a cluster of kids chased each other around a stop sign, swatted each other with books. A boy walked by carrying a trumpet case. Rosalie passed again.

"As cold as it is," Mary Em said, "nobody should be out who doesn't have to be out. The radio said ice this morning. She could—"

A camellia bush rubbed against the house, shook in the wind. If there was a hard freeze tonight, the blossoms would be killed, turn brown and rot on the stems.

"There won't be any blooms." Lov shook the bowl of pecan halves.

"If you're planning to make fruitcakes, they should have been done weeks ago."

"I know." Lov held a large nutmeat shaped like a skinny heart. "I'm planning to make fudge and leave the nuts whole. That makes it twice as luxurious."

"Fudge." Mary Em wiped dust off the table with the side of her hand. "Don't leave any lying around here." Rich chocolate stuff. She could taste it thinking about it, so good, the sweetness melting down her throat. Inches added to her like another layer of clothes. "Give it away," Mary Em snapped. "And remember whose money paid for the sugar and stuff that went into it."

Lov's faded blue eyes darkened. "Why, Tigee—"

Mary Em hadn't been called her baby name in years. She kept sweeping dust with her hand.

"You know I'd put both our names on the gift enclosure." Lov emptied hulls from her lap into the wastebasket.

She's never gained a pound, Mary Em thought, taking the wastebasket to the back porch. And those long skirts she wears, the fringed things—all my friends talk. Why can't she wear pantsuits like the rest of us? Why does she have to be so fancy?

"That woman needs help." Lov stood by the window now.

"Sent off." Mary Em washed her hands.

"No, they don't do that any more. People aren't institutionalized so much these days. Why add strange surroundings, uproot them when there's no need. She's suffering pain as real as any disease."

"She didn't show her grief." Mary Em wiped an already clean counter. "That's what some said who went in when the boy died." Jimmy Ritchie was killed last spring, only a few months after the family moved here. He was pushed, they said fell, down a stairwell, hit his head and died. Weak blood vessel. The doctors said it would have happened anytime. Mary Emmett had seen the stretcher carried out the glass doors of the school, slid into the quiet ambulance. She knew somebody was dead when Charlie Swanner didn't burn his red light, blow the siren. He'd do it for the least reason, especially after he first got the job driving the ambulance. Maybe it got old for him.

"It's like she's pacing," Lov said. "That's so frightening."

People said Rosalie Ritchie never shed a tear, at least not where anybody could see her, but went on with that funeral like it was all somebody else's child. Then when school started back this fall, here she came every day with a look on her face like she didn't know what world she was in.

Lov dropped the drapery. "Let's invite her in. She needs something hot—tea."

Mary Em was a coffee person herself. Before Lov came she kept a pot always hot on the back of the stove. Now it was a fat teakettle for hot water. Lov drank odd teas, ones she ordered in tins from companies that kept sending her brochures, catalogs showing all kinds of expensive things. Things people could get along perfectly well without. Mary Emmett always had and she didn't think she'd missed much.

Lov tapped the window. "Maybe I can get her attention now that everyone's gone. If she'll just look this way . . ."

Mary Em put the kettle on, clicked the button to HI.

Lov lifted her skirt, started toward the enclosed porch. "I'll just—"

"I'll go." Mary Em pushed past her sister, slammed the kitchen door so hard the glass rattled and the wreath kept banging against it like a muffled clock striking.

"Mrs. Ritchie," Mary Em called. "Dear—" She waved across the street to the woman walking.

Finally the woman glanced in Mary Em's direction. "Can you come—?" Mary Em yelled.

The woman stepped off the curb, started stiffly toward her, and slipped into the path of a blue Page's Delivery truck cruising the wrong way down the one-way street.

"Watch . . . out," Mary Em called. "Do be . . . careful."

The truck screamed to a stop, past the crushed rag doll of a woman, who lay in her red coat with her arms and legs at odd angles, anxious eyes frozen in her face.

"It's—" Mary Em put her hands over her face.

"—not your fault." Lov came up behind her, laid her arm across Mary Em's shoulders, drew her close.

They were standing there when the first faint scream of the teakettle started and got shrill, hurting louder.

The Pink Bed

THILDALEE TOLD RONNIE she had to have her bed. Just had to have it. She sat cross-legged on the edge of the tub, smoking. She'd gone three nights without sleeping, two weeks before that of light and fitful sleep. It was beginning to show. Bags under her eyes were dark as pansy petals. And she felt wrung out, limp, like an old T-shirt used to mop with, flung across the clothesline, sour and dry.

"Over my dead body," Ronnie said. "You know that's what it will be. No way I'm going into another man's house when he's not home and steal his furniture." Ronnie shaved without looking in the mirror. With his cheeks and neck soaped he looked like an old man with a white beard. Is that the way he'd look when he got old? Thildalee didn't want to think about that now. That night when she had met Ronnie in the diner and gone back to his motel, she'd thought he had more muscles than anyone she'd ever seen. "Driving a Cat every day for fifteen years will make you or break you," he said.

"What makes you say it's his furniture?" She reached for a Q-tip, poked her ear. "I'll have you know that's my bed. Always has been, always will be. I can't sleep right in anything else."

"Seems to me anybody who's up and down as much as you are every night don't need a bed anyway."

"That's what I'm trying to tell you." She threw her cigarette butt in the commode. "I can't sleep without my bed."

"Aw come on, Sugar Foot." He reached around, tweaked her toe. "You know it's not the bed anyway—it's who's in it."

"Ouch," she said.

"That didn't hurt one bit. You're the touchiest thing I've ever seen in the mornings. A regular old cactus puss."

"You'd be touchy too, if you didn't sleep."

"Get your mind on something else," Ronnie said twenty minutes later when he left for work, coffee mug in one hand, lunchbox in the other. "It ain't going to happen. Not by me anyway."

She leaned out the door for his kiss. He smelled like some spice she remembered as being Christmasy . . . that and orange. He smelled like her father. That made her throat ache, her chest tighten.

He raced the motor, plowed the dust-colored pick-up in a cloud down the road.

"Get your mind on something else," she mimicked, pulled on jeans and a black Coors sweatshirt, hung her nightgown on a hook in the bathroom. That red plastic hook was one of the things she'd added to the doublewide since they bought it. There wasn't much you could add. Everything came as a package, furniture, curtains, shades; Ronnie made them throw in the pictures on the wall, silk flowers on the coffee table, mugs and ceramic canister set in the kitchen. He bought the display model and by durn he wanted it delivered just like he saw it or he'd take his money somewhere it was good.

"Oh, it's good here," the sweating salesman had said. "Right here." Three days later everything was delivered. That was two weeks ago and every night Thildalee slept less. All Ronnie could talk about was that kingsize bed and the bathroom with two tubs and all those mirrors. All she thought about was her bed—her pink upholstered heart-shaped headboard she'd had since she was twelve. Her daddy made it for his little girl. He'd cut out the wood and had it upholstered in the brightest pink marbled plastic she could find. "Don't you think it's bright?" Mama asked. "Yes, ma'am," Thildalee answered. "And that's what I want. Exactly what I want." It was a prettier bed than any movie star had, Marilyn Monroe or Elizabeth Taylor or anybody. When she added white eyelet spread and pillows the whole thing looked like a valentine.

Deane never minded her bed. "You sleep with me," she said the first night they came back from Myrtle Beach. "You sleep in my bed." He smiled, reached to turn back the spread. Never said a word. Deane was as easy-going as anything—at first. So how come in three years a man could change so much? Day and night, there was that much difference to him. One day she was all he ever wanted, the next he came in and cried all over her nightgown. But not until after she'd called every cop in town. They knew. Had a running list. Kept it quiet and took their Christmas bonus every year like they'd earned it.

Ronnie wasn't going to help, Thildalee could see that as she cranked the Mustang. First car she'd ever owned, only car she wanted to own. Her daddy had rebuilt it, repainted it new blue, the works. Let her pick out the seats.

At least there was Mama, Thildalee thought as the Mustang's muffler popped and roared. She'd have to tell Ronnie again how her muffler was acting. Trouble was he wouldn't hear her. "I might as well tell the table," she thought.

Mama was putting out tomato plants in the garden. She straightened up, dusted her hands on her hips. "You would come when I finished," she said. "Ten minutes earlier and I'd let you set out the last half-dozen. Make sure you haven't forgotten how."

Thildalee and Deane never had a garden. Mama gave her a tomato plant to put in a whiskey barrel once. Thildalee planted petunias and the tomato plant got crowded out. Plus it got the wilt, blossom-end rot, droops, white mites, black spot, everything a plant could get. "You spray things," Mama said. "Any fool can grow one tomato plant."

"Not this one," Thildalee said.

In the kitchen Mama handed her a glass of iced tea, took a long drink from her own, tilted back her head, said, "Ahhhh, I needed that."

"I need a favor," Thildalee said. She wanted lemon, but she wasn't going to ask for it. "My bed's still at Deane's."

"So?" Mama said. "What else is new? Any woman who takes off in the middle of the night wearing nothing but her nightgown and not taking a stitch with her, left more than her bed behind."

"I don't care about all the other stuff," Thildalee said. "Besides, Deane put everything that had my name on it in a mini-warehouse. I can go get it any time I want. He told me so."

"Maybe the bed's in that."

"I checked," Thildalee said. "You think I'd come asking if I hadn't?"

"I think you'd better leave well enough alone. What do you want the old thing for? It's never been pretty. Your daddy didn't get the sides even. Left side was always higher."

"It's mine," Thildalee said, "and I just want it." She ended up leaving her glass on the table. Any other time she'd put it in the dishwasher, but today she wasn't doing one thing for people who refused to do a single thing to help her. Wouldn't lift a finger. If her daddy was alive, he'd help and they'd have that bed out of Deane's house, loaded on somebody's truck, and be down the highway before now. Two months ago, one morning at the mill, they said her daddy took a coffee break, went to sit on the stoop in the sun, and just kept sitting there. When somebody thought to call him, he was dead. Heart attack. "Went in a wink," the doctor said. "He never knew a thing."

Thildalee drove around awhile, through the square, past all the empty-eyed stores downtown, past the new shopping center with a big J.C. Penney's and Rose's just completed. Maybe she'd get a job selling lingerie at Penney's. That might be something she'd like. She imagined herself unpacking all lacy and silky things, easing and patting them onto hangers.

She cruised by her old high school where everybody seemed to be in class or out doing gym on the athletic field. She bet old Miss Wilkins was still teaching Home Management, making those girls bake cakes from scratch when the minute they got out of her lab, they'd buy all the mixes they could get their hands on.

She and Deane met in Home Management. He was the one who baked the best coconut cakes in the whole world. That and the fact he could iron must have had something to do with her marrying him. His shirt collars always looked so smooth she wanted to press her cheek against them. And he smelled clean, like soap and starch and sheets when her mama dried them on the line in summer.

Thildalee parked across the street from the drugstore, went in and ordered a fountain Coke, sat in a back booth carved with the names of everybody from Eatonsville. There was probably Adam Loves Eve, that booth was so old. She traced carved hearts and arrows, initials, nicknames . . . Who was Pep? And Duck Frommer? Crazy Legs? Why did girls never have nicknames? Maybe it was all jock and locker room jokes anyway. Girls in locker rooms spent all their time taking showers, shampooing hair, blowdrying and hot-combing. Maybe hair made the difference.

She finished her Coke, bought a bottle of some new sham-

41

poo called "Sure Enough"—which sounded more like a deodorant—and left.

She cruised by her old neighborhood . . . just in case. She didn't know in case what, but just in case. The Bakers still hadn't fixed their smashed mailbox. The dead pines in Miller's yard weren't down, just looked browner, more dead. Tony Braswell's bike lay flung next to the street where anybody could steal it in a second. If they wanted the rusty old thing. Maybe nobody did.

And Deane's car was in the drive. What was he doing home in the middle of the morning? Was he sick? She started to pull in behind it, go in. She still had her key. Instead she decided to drive around the block. Maybe he took a day off to do errands, take the dog in to be clipped, do the laundry, shampoo the rug, go to an afternoon movie. Sometimes he took a sick day to do those things. Not that the company ever found out. They'd have a fit. Him out hosing off his car when he was supposed to be in bed with the "bug." But usually those were half-days he took, not mornings. Not unless he really was sick.

She rounded the corner when she saw the two of them come out, smiling and walking all hugged up. It was sickening. Two adults acting so icky. That's all you could call it, sickening . . . icky. Lucky Thildalee was going slow so she could pull in the Braswells' empty carport, get the Mustang out of the way before Deane spotted it. Not that he was looking at anything but that guy, whoever he was, all long-legged in short shorts cut up at the thigh. Not the kind of thing a decent person wore out the door. Shorts like that might be right for some workout club or the YMCA, but you didn't go around in public for everybody to see everything you had—unless you were advertising.

Deane didn't even open his car for his "friend." Both of them got in on the driver's side and stayed stuck together as he backed out.

That's when Thildalee made her move. She was out of

Braswell's and parked across her own drive, blocked Deane's car before he got it in reverse good.

"What's all this about?" He got out and came around her window after he stopped honking and saw who she was.

"It's about my bed," she said.

"What about your bed?"

"I want it," she said.

"Is that all?" He ran his hand through his uncombed hair. She noticed he looked grayer than two months ago. Or maybe he was then and she didn't see it. "Thildalee, you just take anything you want in that house—except my exercise bike. That's new and I want it for the condo."

"Condo?" she said weakly.

"At Jim's place. They got a pool, tennis courts." He bent to tie his shoe. New Reeboks, she noticed. "I was going to call you. The yard sale's Saturday."

"Oh," Thildalee said, and moved her car to let him leave. The blond boy waved, friendly as anything. Bleached, Thildalee thought, and too skinny. He looked like a stalk; a sunflower.

She watched in her rearview mirror until there wasn't a trace of a taillight. That was all there was to it, she thought as she let herself in the kitchen. His dishes were still in the sink. *Their* dishes were still in the sink. Jim must have spent the night. "Well," Thildalee said to the walls. "He didn't even let my side of the bed get cold before he's got somebody hopping in it."

That was all right, she told herself, and a little catch of her breath echoed in the still house. That was perfectly fine. All she wanted was her bed.

The house smelled like cigarettes. She opened the den window on her way to the bedroom. There was half a bottle of vodka on the coffee table, two glasses, some sort of sticky green dip and taco chips. She looked away.

She dreaded seeing the bed. Unmade beds always bothered her. She'd never left one unmade behind in her life. Not even on their honeymoon. Deane kept saying that's what they had maids for and why did she have to be so prissy. And she said she wasn't prissy at all. It was just one of the things her mother taught her. Always make your bed. He finally thought it was cute. He just didn't think it was cute the way she never wiped the shower after she finished, never turned the hot water completely off, and wouldn't drink a Coke from anything but a bottle or glass. "They taste like the can," she said. But that wasn't why she left. Not that Mama nor Patsy or anybody else would ever understand. "You got the perfect husband," they all said. "I could stay married forever to someone who does all the cooking, food shopping and cleans the house the way Deane does. You just don't know how good you got it." She knew. But cooking and cleaning wasn't what marriage was all about. She'd like to tell Miss Wilkins a thing or two now.

The first thing Thildalee noticed when she got to the bedroom was the perfectly made bed. Her white eyelet spread and pillows, ruffles all in place. That was when she began to cry. And cry and cry. She cried until she hiccuped. Her face was hot and she looked for something to wipe it. She saw something under the bed and reached for it. One of her old terrycloth scuffs. On her knees, she looked for the other and saw only dust bunnies, a curling paperback book, and a pencil with a broken point.

She wiped her face with her hands, straightened up, tucked the bedroom shoe in the back pocket of her jeans, and walked out, closing the door with a small click that sounded like the echo of one last hiccup.

Daisy Wars

I HAVE ARGUED with that woman and argued with that woman. But when she gets Shasta Daisies planted in her brain, there's no uprooting them.

"They fall over," I told her. Little spindly things. Nothing to them but a stem and blotch of fuzz. She won't hear it.

"Therma Ann," I said, "you're going to split the garden club right down the middle. You're going to turn friend against friend, neighbor against neighbor, and preacher against preacher." She won't hear it. Goes traipsing around to the Lions Club, the Wednesday Night Men's Fish Fry, and who knows what-all with her little rolled-up drawings. Loves for them to say what a wonderful job the ladies in this town are doing to make it a better place to live. Acts like she thought of it all by herself and is doing it single-handed. That garden club has been selling Chocolate Nut Crumbles and Pecan Pralines-in-a-Can for the last six months. Fronnie Laidlorn is so mad now she's not speaking to half the members. Said they knew when they voted she'd never been able

45

to resist chocolate in any shape nor form. They made her drop Weight Watchers. Said they saw she was losing and couldn't stand it. I said the rest of them could have sold candy; she didn't have to. Nobody held her arms and made her. I tried to get them to order stationery. It's harder to sell but not impossible, I said. They said it wasn't something people had to have and there wouldn't be repeat orders. And besides, nobody in this town wrote letters anyway. I said well, why don't we just close down the post office too, but nobody heard me.

This town is dead enough as it is. We don't need any more empty buildings to sit and watch run down. If it wasn't for the bank, drugstore, hardware, and Baptist church, we could just close up shop. Strike Eddysville off the map—if it's on any. I'm the only business still open on my side of the street and it's awful. Those empty stores attract mice and who knows what all slips in from the back alley?

I remember when this town had four hardwares, an FCX, and six churches. There was a dress store in every block, three dimestores and more shoe stores than you could get into on a Saturday, if you tried on a pair each place. I have known Saturdays when you had to park a mile from the square. When you saw everybody—neighbors, cousins, preachers, people you hadn't seen since the last funeral.

One shopping center will ruin a county, I've always heard. They put in a chain department store, drugstore, and hamburger drive-in, run the local businesses out. Joe's Grill had been on the lot behind the jail for twenty-five years. Wasn't big enough to stump your toe in, but Joe could cook with his eyes closed. He made the best fried sandwiches in town. I ate one every day of my life as long as he was in business, except Sundays, and then when I had a funeral. Ten o'clock sharp, Joe would send whoever happened to be passing around with my order. Half the time he'd throw in a fried pie. I don't know how that man stayed in business. Sometimes I don't know how any of us does, with the way people in this town like to take their business elsewhere. Not to the one who is your neighbor and best friend and does the job at half the price, but for no reason. Whim. Fickle. I have had to face the truth that people will listen to somebody talk a fast streak and smile a lot even if she is wearing a five-year-old hundred-percent polyester dress most of us threw out years ago. Mine was made from the same pattern, Simplicity #6066, but I pushed it to the back of my closet and forgot it. Some people don't keep up, won't keep up, whether it's clothes or other things. I say if they don't *see* fashion, how can they see something as complicated as landscape design? That's what this boils down to—simple landscape design.

Not many towns this size have two entrances and one exit. You have to keep that in mind. Marigolds, I said. You can depend on marigolds. Nothing touches them. Not dry weather, not rot, not mildew, not mealybugs. I've worked in flowers all my life and I know my Abelia, my Pittosporum, my hollies, and my Buxus from a name on the page. Why can't people trust a trained eye? I know daisies and design. I *see* them. And trouble at the same time.

Every year I take two days off, close my shop and go the Convention. No telling how much business I lose. Don't anybody die the second week in July, I tell people. Because Lallah Carpenter won't be here to help you out. I gas my station wagon, run up motel bills you wouldn't believe, and come back with it loaded to the rims.

I see to it personally that people in this town hold their heads up with the best of them when it comes to weddings and funerals. I was the first to go with artificial flowers—nobody called them that but those of us in the floral industry—and they almost took over. Silk flowers? When they started, I filled my shelves with every color rose and carnation made; blue, black, and orange if they wanted them. I was the first to make bridal bouquets in silk flowers for "keeping" and I've looked the other way when some have been used twice.

47

I know how to put on a wedding. People give me credit for that. Women who wouldn't speak to you if you ran over them in the streets will come calling when their Janie or Mona Rae or Louine starts thinking wedding. Asking what dates I have open. I got lace cloths and secret wedding punch recipes nobody can touch. And I have sugar flowers put on my wedding cakes. Those little bride-and-grooms are overdone, I tell my people. Flowers are my middle name. Sometimes I dream them all night long. Arrange them in my sleep, take orders and deliver. It's not a business you can let go at the end of a day.

Especially the funeral part. After the preacher, I'm the next to know. And I do a good job. Nobody has ever said they didn't get their money's worth on a neighborhood wreath. There are families in this town who won't let a permanent arrangement in their door. And those who welcome them for every holiday in the year. People appreciate your knowing things like that.

My sweet daddy-in-law had a yard full of flowers. Plus every houseplant you could name.

"You could start a business," Daddy Bell said one morning, making his way to the breakfast table. We always drank coffee together. That was the one thing he taught me. I'd never touched a drop in my life until I married Tom Bell and he brought his daddy to live with us. Now I can't do without it. Can't find one hand with the other until I have my first cup. So Daddy Bell was the one who started me off. And this business has been running nights, days, and weekends ever since.

Everybody in the garden club said I was the one with the natural green thumb. For a while I thought of calling myself that, but it sounded too much plants and shrubs and nursery. So I ended up with "Budding Beauty" because I could see the *B*'s with two big loops.

I can *see* things. That's what I tried to tell the garden club after their civic beautification committee came calling—

after they'd asked Therma Ann to draw up their plans. If they'd come to me first I could have saved a lot of heartache and heartbreak. But no, they go to Therma Ann. Let her make some little chicken scratches on paper, put color over them and get everybody excited.

For somebody who never had a single art lesson in her life, she does draw a straight line. With a ruler. And the brick entrance-way with "Welcome to Eddysville" looked good when you thought how bare that place was now.

Highway 701 is not your heavily traveled road. Thank goodness, I say. But it is two-lane and paved and we have a stoplight.

There wasn't an evergreen in the plan, but did I point that out? I did not. I was the soul of sweetness. They said bricks had been donated and Therma's husband offered to lay them free. I said be sure he works on a day when he's . . . ah . . . feeling well. I did not mention his drinking habits which everyone knows. And if you don't watch him every minute—stand right out there—then you'll get a wall crooked as that bend in the road to the river.

And little gas lamps? Donated too. Weren't they tickled? I asked if anyone had considered electricity? Something not quite so eternal, but which could be turned on and off. They have lights burning all the time and while it may look friendly and "welcome to our town"–ish, somebody will complain. They will cry taxpayers' money, even when it's not.

Too late to change their minds, I could see that. All them acting like hens on a nest of Easter eggs. Jelly beans, I started to say, but didn't. Wasn't going to shoot off my mouth to anybody who would listen. Those things come home to sit on your mantel and roost. Therma Ann ought to know.

She was the one calling the baby premature when it came two months too soon. Nine pounds? All along I said it didn't matter if things were hurried up. Of course I wanted Tommy Lee to finish school before marriage, maybe take a course or two in auto mechanics if he wanted, but I have learned with children what you want and what you get aren't always the same things. I said boys will be boys, especially if girls let them. Make the best of it I said when they told me. You weren't the first and you won't be the last. It's nothing to be ashamed of, nothing new since Adam and Eve.

I was the one who insisted on a church wedding though. Every girl needs a memory like that in the back of her life, I told Rita.

It will mean more to you as time passes. And Tommy Lee agreed when I mentioned the showers for Rita and bachelor party for him. He didn't mind waiting a few weeks until we could get things in the works. I think he'd still be waiting if it was up to him. But he's like me. We make the best of things and more.

I mean how many mothers of the groom do you know, who plan, direct, and pay for the whole wedding? While Therma Ann is in the background the whole time pushing them to go across the state line to Cheraw so she can fudge the date a little if she has to. And she did. She was scared to death Rita would show walking down the aisle. She wouldn't have been the first. I expect to see bridal gowns in the maternity shops any day now. It wasn't anything the town didn't already know. Out in the open, I've always said. That's the way I've been. The only way to be.

When my first husband up and left and little Tommy not but two, I told it. Good riddance I said. Then when Charlie Flaggle was dying with his trouble I told it. We didn't keep it to ourselves even if trade did fall off at the barber shop. Picked up some afterwards and stayed steady until he couldn't hold the trimmers and got to nicking too many ears. Nobody cut hair like him. Three generations in the same barber shop. I even thought Tommy Lee might take it up, but it's too much indoors all the time for him. Gilda made the best beauty shop there though . . . those mirrors down one wall and that old pole out front. She cuts men and women. Only store open in that whole block. "We are in the same boat," I tell her, "and no beautification project is going to change a thing."

Try telling that to Therma Ann. I would if it wouldn't mean breaking my word not to speak to her again. Six weeks next Sunday. I said it and slammed the door. Billy is her grandson same as mine. Or more. If you go back and look at some things. I never let my son go swinging his hips up and down the streets of this town in cut-off jeans so short they showed what they were supposed to cover. Little terry tops no bigger than a washcloth and everything spilled out. Advertising. I never claimed my son was any stronger nor weaker than a regular man. Make the most, I said, but it was a marriage he was caught into. Trapped. At least he hasn't gone running home every time somebody turned their face upside down at him.

"Make your bed," I said. "You sleep in it." And he has. If Rita's mama had been home showing and telling her a thing or two, not running around from club to club, she might be holding her end of a marriage up.

Park benches. That's what Therma wants now. For the vacant lot where Miller's Drugstore stood for fifty years. She'd got them drawn into her plan. That's one thing I agree with her about. If she's bound and determined to plant the lot, then I'll help her with them. If people are sitting, they can't be parading around, showing all they've got. I give Therma Ann credit where credit is due. But I will fight her until the Fourth of July on Shasta Daisies. I know my flowers.

As my sweet daddy-in-law used to say, "Lallah, you got more wheels in the road than anybody I know." And I don't intend to let somebody in a five-year-old polyester dress with Shasta Daisies on the brain run the show.

Wooden Apples

THE OLD CEDAR made a dark triangle of shade. Patsy had spread her quilt in the widest part so close to the tree she smelled its spiced clean scent. When she closed her eyes she smelled it stronger, but she hadn't made a pallet in the yard to sleep, just read.

In August no place was cool, but the cedar shade was cooler than the house and there was an occasional breeze.

She heard her brothers' voices from the kitchen. "Rat. You stinko. You're not playing fair and I'm going to tell." They played Monopoly, fought over Boardwalk and Park Place, who got the railroads and utilities. They were mad at first when she wouldn't play, wanted to take a quilt and go outside. Then they forgot about her.

She was almost asleep when someone said, "Wish I had nothing to do all day but take a nap in the shade." Ladella Honeycutt leaned over her.

Ladella lived across the street. She was tall and blonde, tanned in white short shorts and some fluffy pink halter top.

She had pink hoops in her ears and smelled like warm straw-berries. Her nails were much too long and perfect for anyone who did much in the house, Mama said, yet when she strolled her baby in the evenings both of them looked fresh and clean. "She just does it to show her legs," Mama said once. Patsy helped her snap beans. They sat on the back porch. It was late on a Saturday afternoon and Mama wanted to get the canner on before she started supper. It would be the third canning of beans she'd done this week. When she made the remark about Ladella, Patsy looked up. It didn't sound like Mama saying that. There was an edge to her voice. "Some people wouldn't know a fresh vegetable if it ran up and jumped in their face." Mama tossed a handful of snapped beans in the flat metal pan between them.

Patsy thought Ladella ever so beautiful. "That hair's not real," Mama said. "It's bleached—p'roxided—whatever they do."

Patsy didn't care. She wanted to be tall and blonde even if it wasn't real and have a sweet baby like David to play pat-a-cake with, push up and down the street in his stroller.

"If there was anything much to her," Mama said, "her husband would live with her—if there is one."

That was the mystery. If Ladella had a husband she never mentioned it, and when Patsy babysat David at night, La-della always left and came back by herself. "Maybe she's divorced," Patsy said. "Maybe her husband's dead."

"Maybe there never was one," Mama said.

Patsy couldn't imagine anyone who wouldn't want to marry Ladella, have a baby like David who hugged everyone, laughed, and went to sleep quietly sucking his thumb. She'd never heard him cry.

"Can you babysit Saturday night?" Ladella asked.

"Where's David?" Patsy looked around.

"Asleep," Ladella said. "He's teething and didn't get his nap out this morning. I've got the fan on him and he's sleep-ing like a baby." She laughed. "But then he always does, doesn't he? I mean what else could he sleep like?" She turned over the book Patsy had on the blanket. "I've read this. Want me to tell you how it ends?"

"Don't you dare." Patsy snatched back her book. She knew how it ended. Happily ever after. All the books did, but somehow she didn't quite know until she got there.

"Hey, gorgeous." Patsy's father came down the back porch steps. "I'd been home early if I knew I had two beautiful girls waiting for me in my back yard."

Ladella laughed, pushed back her hair. She spread her legs on the blanket, wiggled her toes in their white patent sandals. "How do you like my new nail polish?" she asked. "It's called Cherry Smash."

"I like it," Patsy's father said. "Looks good enough to eat." He reached for one of Ladella's feet.

"I meant Patsy," she said. "I was asking Patsy how she liked it."

Patsy didn't know her father knew Ladella well enough to tease and talk like that. He'd only seen her a few times when she came in to borrow a stick of butter or something. She'd lived on Harper Street a few months. Moved in the last of May, a week or so before school was out. David was three months old, a really little baby, and she didn't leave him then. Patsy had sat with him a few times or so and mostly when he was already in bed. She only had to check him, be there to change him if he woke, heat a bottle if he cried. He never had. And Ladella always paid her ten dollars a time, plus a tip when she washed the dishes soaking in the sink. About a week's worth of dishes, Patsy thought. She couldn't stand to be in the house with that many sticky dishes. That's the real reason she washed them and the baby was asleep. There was no TV and she was bored. Ladella gave her five dollars for washing the dishes. "It was worth every cent," she said the first time, and lit a cigarette, slipped off her shoes, and slid down on the couch. She wore the same nail polish then, Patsy remembered. It wasn't new. So why had she said so?

Her father teased Ladella some more about her tan, how he bet she had it all over and she acted like she didn't know what he was talking about. Said she didn't have any tan at all compared to how dark she used to get going to the beach and she hadn't been to the beach forever. "A couple of lifetimes ago," she said.

Patsy wanted her father to be in a good mood. She had been asked to go to the movies with Linda. Linda's mother would pick her up, bring her back a little after nine. Patsy had money to pay for her ticket. All her father had to do was say it was okay and stay home with her brothers until she got back. She didn't know if he'd do it. Her mother worked nights in the sock mill, going in at three and coming home after eleven. She said those machines turned out millions of socks; enough socks for every man, woman, child, cat, and dog in the world to never have to go barefooted again. She said they spit socks out faster than you could catch them and cut the threads.

Patsy had to make supper for her father and two brothers. Usually she heated things left from lunch—garden vegetables, cornbread and biscuits—peeled tomatoes and cucumbers, put vinegar over them.

In the summer her father grew enough vegetables to give half the county. Her mother said she didn't care if those people he gave it to would come help hoe and pick it when it got ready. Those were the hard parts. Corn her father planted was now so tall she couldn't see across where Ladella lived unless she stood.

Patsy smoothed a wrinkle from the blanket and asked her father about the movies.

"You hear that?" He cocked his head at Ladella. "My little girl's going on a date."

"Not a date, Daddy," she said. "It's with Linda. You know Linda. Her mother's going to take us."

"Skinny kid with the braces and big ears?" he said. "Looks

like somebody left her out in the rain."

"Daddy," Patsy said, "she's my friend. She's nice and her mother's nice and—"

"I guess you can go," he said, "if you put on a skirt."

"Bring a brush and I'll comb your hair for you," Ladella said.

Patsy ran, pulled a dress from the hanger and over her head. The dress felt still warm from her mother's iron, though she knew it couldn't be, and smelled like soap and sunshine. She grabbed a brush and comb, flew down the hall and back steps. She was afraid Ladella hadn't meant to comb her hair at all and would be gone to check on David.

Ladella was still there, talking to Patsy's father, who laughed, showed all his teeth. He didn't laugh like that much. Mostly he frowned or yelled they made too much noise or the TV got on his nerves. Then he'd slam down his newspaper and say he was going where he could get some peace.

The service station. That's where Patsy's mother said he went. Once when Patsy knew they needed milk for breakfast she called, asked to speak to him, and he wasn't there. Then someone corrected in the background. "Yeah," the man said, "Roland Lentz was here—till a few minutes ago. He just left. You want to call back? I can give him a message."

She left the message about bringing home milk but the next morning there wasn't any and her father acted mad, said he forgot.

Sometimes he wasn't home when she went to bed. Her brothers had to be in bed at ten, no later, but she could stay up until ten-thirty, take a long bath, have the rest of the hot water all to herself. She'd be almost asleep when her father came quietly in, went straight to bed, not even turning on the lights. Minutes later her mother came from work. Even her footsteps on the porch sounded tired.

Patsy wondered if Ladella ever got tired. She never looked

nor acted it. She took the brush and began on Patsy's hair, giggling about something. Her hands were smooth and Patsy closed her eyes as Ladella brushed. It had been a long time since her mother had time to brush, comb, do pretty things to Patsy's hair, but that was okay. Patsy liked doing things for herself. She'd just forgotten how nice it felt to have someone do things for her. Soothing things.

"Now," Ladella said, "you'll knock 'em dead. You'll be the prettiest girl there." She pulled Patsy's collar from inside the neckband, buttoned the top button. "I've got a cute pin that would look just perfect on that collar," she said. "Let me go check on David and I'll get it."

"I'll go along and look at that water heater for you," Daddy said. He winked at Ladella, who said, "Oh . . . sure. That will be fine."

Patsy watched them walk across the street. Ladella was almost as tall as her father and she walked with a little jiggle, almost a bounce, her hair lifting and falling, her legs almost gliding over asphalt, grass.

Patsy folded the blanket, was starting toward the house when Ladella called from her door. "I found it. Come let me pin it on."

"I'll bring it back in the morning," Patsy said as Ladella patted the red wooden apple pin in place on her collar.

"Oh, no need for that. You keep it. I want you to have it."

"Thank you," Patsy said, and took the blanket in, set places for supper, and listened for Linda's mother to toot the car horn.

When she came in from the movie, her father wasn't home, and his plate was still clean on the table.

The next morning when her mother woke her she picked up Patsy's dress, started to hang it up, and saw the wooden apple pin. "Where'd this come from?" she asked.

"Ladella," Patsy yawned. "She gave it to me."

"When?" Mama closed the closet door.

"Yesterday . . . on the blanket . . . when she came over."

"Over here?" her mother said. "Where was the baby?"

"Oh, he was asleep," Patsy said. "And Daddy went to fix her hot water heater. He said I could go to the movies with Linda. Her mother picked us up."

Mama took the pin off the dress. "I don't think you better keep this. She's not a very nice person."

"But I like her," Patsy said. "She's nice to me."

"She's nice to a lot of people," Mama said. "A little nicer than she's supposed to be. I think Miss Ladella's middle name is trouble."

The pin left a rusty mark on the collar of Patsy's dress. It didn't even wash out. Mama and Daddy talked a long time the next Sunday afternoon. Sometimes her mother cried. Sometimes her father yelled. Then he finally left. Patsy and her mother and brothers had supper alone, but that was nothing new. Her mother red-eyed, not saying much. Not making jokes over toasted cheese and milk, nothing.

Sometime during the night, her father came home. It was late, but Patsy was awake, thinking. She thought it was funny how you could live in the same house with four other people and not know much about them. Not know them at all. How you found out little things you didn't really want to know, things that hurt and made you worry if the world was all right. And how her brothers could sleep and play and sometimes argue and fight and not know anything at all.

Across the Bridge

LYNNE HAD READ to him all night. "And the wicked old troll called, 'Who goes trip-tropping across my bridge?'" She read with her eyes closed; the print felt raised on her eyelids as she sing-songed the words. "'It is I, the littlest Billy Goat Gruff, who goes trip-tropping across the bridge.'"

At times when she thought Danny asleep, Lynne stopped reading. He'd cry, "Read, Mama, read!" in such a shrill, feeble voice it hurt to hear him.

So she read, every book they had brought to the hospital, every book she could remember reading Danny; sang songs in a voice she tried to make steady; and said rhymes, "One, two, buckle my shoe." She stopped, then went stumbling on. Danny's scuffed shoes were in the metal locker at the foot of the bed. The day they brought Danny to the hospital, he asked a dozen times for his clothes, to see his shoes. She took them from his locker, held his shoes, jeans, and brown jacket so he could see them. Later, when his eyes swelled shut, he stopped asking for his clothes and begged for a blanket; he was cold, so cold. But she couldn't give him a blanket. Not even a sterile sheet was allowed to touch his raw body. Finally he curled into a fetal position and withdrew inside his cocoon of pain-killing drugs. Her voice was the only link between that world and the hospital room. Her voice and the bottle of blood draining slowly into his veins from an umbilical cord to a machine. The machine throbbed its desperate rhythm. Lynne wanted to cry faster, faster.

Toward morning Danny dozed and Lynne stopped reading but didn't move from her chair beside his bed. Sometimes she sipped warm water to ease her dry throat. Fluids. The doctors said Danny was losing all his body fluids and there was nothing they could do. When the pairs of doctors came and went, mumbling behind masks, she read bewilderment in their eyes. "When these wonder drugs backfire . . ." they murmured. Danny had had measles, then a strep throat. Dr. Barger gave him penicillin as he had before. Only this time it reacted. It was like nothing anyone had ever seen before. "We don't know what to do," the doctors said. "What to do."

When Jim came, Lynne was sitting in the rocking chair, her arms wrapped tight around herself to keep them from swinging empty as the chair thumped back and forth on the cold tile floor. He touched her shoulder, walked to the crib, and stood quietly like someone paying respects. Lynne closed her eyes, leaned back. From behind, Jim stroked her hair. Danny used to do that sometimes. She squeezed herself tighter. Jim's voice was low. "No change?"

Lynne shook her head. "None." She stood, hands on the chair back, and Jim pulled her close. His raincoat was damp, smelled of the outdoors. How much older Jim looked, as though this hospital week had been years that wore his face long and sad.

He drew tight lines on his forehead. "Honey, you have got to get some rest. Go home for a little while."

"I can't. I can't leave Danny."

"You've got to. You're going to make yourself sick." He

took her coat from the locker. "Put this on. It's raining out." He slid her arms into the coat, buttoned it all the way down, as she used to do for Danny. Then Jim took a scarf, tied it under her chin, tried to laugh at his big, slow fingers, and in the dresser found her purse, closed her fingers around its leather edge. "Now, go." He opened the door, gave her a small shove. "The car is in the A parking lot."

Lynne gripped the door facing. "When Danny wakes . . . if he asks for me, tell him I'll be right back."

"I will," Jim whispered, closed the door.

In the hall, Lynne waited for an elevator until she realized she hadn't pushed the button. Running, she took the stairs and her shoes made loud, hollow echoes as though someone followed. One more turn, she rounded the corner, to the glass doors, then parking lot.

Lynne felt for her car keys. A lock of hair tickled her cheek as she started the car. She pushed her hair back and across a wet cheek. It was rain. She wouldn't cry, she wouldn't break down.

She eased the car into an almost deserted street, reminded herself to turn on the wipers and drive slowly. Red traffic lights blinked their scared doe eyes as she drove. Main Street, Greenway, past the A&P, then home.

In the driveway, she stopped the car and sat, just sat. Cold, she hadn't turned the heater on, stiff and numb. She jumped as rain pelted from the oak tree onto the car. The lowest limb on that tree was Danny's. He bounced on it, played "horse," cowboy hat sideways on his head.

Quickly Lynne slammed the door and ran up the walk. There was a light in the kitchen and Mother Grogan, Jim's mother, sat at the bar. Jim had driven to Bolton for his mother to come care for the baby the day they took Danny to the hospital. The day the blisters—huge water balloons— formed all over Danny. And broke, leaving him raw. Never saw anything like it, the doctors said. The nurses' eyes grew soft and misty as they looked at him.

Lynne blinked, tugged off her scarf, coat.

Mother Grogan stopped turning the newspaper. "You scared me for a minute. I didn't hear the car. Where's Jim?"

"At the hospital with Danny." Lynne laid her things across the empty highchair. This room didn't seem like *her* kitchen anymore. Different, things moved; her planter of Sansevieria on the counter instead of the window, a bowl of fruit atop the refrigerator, a rug she used on the porch spread before the sink.

Mother Grogan stacked a section of the paper. "I didn't hear Jim up or I would've fixed him breakfast. A man shouldn't go around on an empty stomach."

"That's okay," Lynne sat in Jim's chair. "He can eat Danny's breakfast. Danny hasn't been . . ."

"How's Danny? Any change?"

"No." Lynne thumbed corners of the newspapers. "The doctors don't say much. They don't know. It the transfusions can be completed before the vein gives out . . . if his skin would start to heal . . ."

Mother Grogan rattled pans under the stove, found Lynne's coffeepot, filled it. She wore a blue chenille robe Lynne gave her one Christmas. It was almost white now. And Jim's bedroom slippers. They flapped as she walked.

"It took me a while at first to find where you keep things." Mother Grogan held the coffee canister. "I'm used to it now."

She could have borrowed my slippers, Lynne thought. They might be more comfortable. "We appreciate your coming like this, Mother Grogan, taking care of the baby and all. I don't know what we would have done."

"That Eddie." She jammed on the coffeepot lid. "He's the sweetest thing. So good. Don't cry or fuss. Just plays with his granny. It's the most I've ever been around him and I didn't know how he'd take to me, not all the time that is." She clicked the stove button, went to the refrigerator. "He wakes up at the crack of dawn, cooing and carrying on in his bed.

Soon as I get up and give him his bottle, he goes right back to sleep." She took the chair across from Lynne, smoothed her crinkled short hair. "Usually I stay up, but this morning was so bad, rainy, I crawled back in, and was asleep before I knew it."

"Is Edward awake now?" Lynne listened. She heard the crib rattle and ran down the hall to him. "Precious." She hugged the sleeper-clad baby. He smelled of milk, and the strong ammonia of his diapers stung her nose. "Soaked," she said, changing him.

The baby gurgled and pulled at her as she dressed him. Red overalls, striped T-shirt. Danny always said Edward looked like a jack-in-the-box in that outfit. Danny. The drawers where she kept Danny's clothes were tightly shut. Danny.

"Boo." Lynne tickled the baby, tugging on his shoes and socks. She felt guilty. This week all she had thought about was Danny. She'd forgotten Edward. Danny needed her so desperately.

She carried him to the kitchen, hurrying past Danny's too-neat room, toys in a line on his shelves.

At the stove, Mother Grogan waved a spatula. "You sit down. I got some sausage fried and these eggs will be ready in a jiffy."

"Coffee will be fine." Lynne popped the baby in his high chair. "I'm not hungry."

Mother Grogan shoved a plate with two large yellow eyes before Lynne. "Now you eat all that."

The egg eyes glared at her. She never liked eggs and didn't think she could get them down this morning. "I'll feed Edward." She got up. "You eat your breakfast."

"No, I already mixed Eddie's cereal with applesauce. He eats it better that way." Mother Grogan poked the gray matter into Edward's open mouth.

Lynne cut brown rims from her eggs. She wanted to feed the baby. Do that much for her week's neglect.

"Fred's coming today." Mother Grogan scraped a blob from Edward's chin, pushed it back in his mouth. "He said when I left if he didn't hear anything he'd be over Saturday. He must have had a time this week. Doing for himself."

Lynne thought of Jim's father, wide-shouldered, gangling outdoorsman of a fellow in the kitchen, dropping, spilling things.

"Course he could eat over at Estelle's," Mother Grogan went on. "If she ever cooked and he knew when she'd have a meal."

Estelle. Jim's sister. Jim said his sister might have learned to do a few things for herself if his mother hadn't always been right there to do everything for her. Including raise those children.

"I got a letter from Estelle this week. Said she and the kids might come over with Fred." Mother Grogan wiped Edward's face, then laughed. "I bet those kids have sure missed me this week. There's not a day goes by that one of them, Billy, Tina, or the baby ain't over there. Spending the day, the night, half the time. I feel like I've raised those kids *myself*."

Mother Grogan and her old-fashioned way of child-raising. That survival-of-the-fittest business made Lynne's skin crawl. When any neighbor child had measles, mumps, chicken pox, Mother Grogan *took* Estelle's children over to be exposed. Might as well have it and get it over with, she said. Lynne disagreed and Mother Grogan said she was too particular with her children. Always carrying them to the doctor's for things and shots when they weren't sick. Tina had the measles after Mother Grogan's exposing her to a neighborhood child. Danny caught the measles from Tina. Mother Grogan said it wouldn't hurt him and he'd be glad to have them done and over with before he started school. Measles, then strep throat, penicillin, now this . . . God, now this. Oh God.

"I thought since Estelle and the kids was coming"—

Mother Grogan put Edward's dish on the counter—"I'd see if Tina didn't want to stay over here. I've never been away from those kids this long a time. I know it's about to kill them not seeing me every day."

"Sure." Lynne stirred sugar in her coffee. "She would be a lot of company to you and maybe help with the baby." Lynne could see Tina swinging on Danny's swings, her hair blowing in the wind.

Mother Grogan stabbed her eggs, dipped toast in the yellow blood. "Only thing is"—she broke off more toast, chewed loudly—"Estelle won't be planning on Tina staying and she won't have her any extra clothes."

Lynne watched the baby rub his sticky cereal hands in his hair.

"I thought"—Mother Grogan went on eating—"since Tina and Danny are about the same age and he's not much bigger than she is, Tina could wear Danny's clothes. It won't hurt her none to wear boy's clothes for a week."

"What?" Lynne's cup crashed on the saucer, sloshed an ugly stain on the mat. Tina in Danny's shirts and jeans, asleep under his warm blanket. "No," Lynne said quietly, "no." Her shoulders shook in hard jerks and she couldn't stop them. Danny was so cold and he couldn't even have a sheet. And his clothes . . .

"You've always been selfish." Mother Grogan pinched her mouth, made her small eyes hard as dried peas. "Been too particular with your children. Selfish is what."

"No, you don't understand." Lynne gripped the table.

"I understand all right. You don't want Tina wearing Danny's clothes. That's okay. I wouldn't let her touch a thing of Danny's if that's the way you want it."

"No, don't you see?" Lynne reached for Mother Grogan's arm, but she pulled away. "Danny can't . . ." Her eyes blurred. "He can't wear his clothes . . . He's dying." It was the first time she had said the word, allowed it. Now the tears tore loose. The tears she'd held in a week came out in

67

great heaving gasps in the bedroom until she lay there empty. Drained and weak, her head was heavy but she slept a fitful sleep, exhausted. The telephone awoke her and Jim's voice.

"Lynne, honey, are you there?"

"Yes," she said. The spread had left waffle marks on her arms. She felt them on her face. It was dry now.

"Danny has started to heal. The doctors were by and found a place on his back. They think he's going to be okay now."

Healing. The sign they had waited for, watched for. She had begun to think it would never happen.

Danny was going to get well. He would make it.

"They say he's not out of the woods yet, but they're optimistic."

"I'll be there as soon as I can. Tell Danny I'm coming." She hung up the phone.

Mother Grogan stood in the doorway, Edward sagging on her hip. She put him on the floor. "Was it Danny?"

"Jim says the doctors think he's going to make it." Lynne picked up the crawling baby and hugged him. "Your brother is going to be okay." The baby laughed and reached up to pull her hair.

"Did you hear?" She swung the baby and embraced Mother Grogan. "Danny's not going to die."

Mother Grogan began to smooth the bed. Lynne put the baby down and helped her.

"I'm sorry about before," she said. "It's okay for Tina to wear Danny's clothes. I don't care if she wears everything he has."

"No." Mother Grogan's hand was on the doorknob. "I wouldn't think of it." She turned and left the room.

Lynne started after her, then stopped. She felt the baby's diaper. He needed to be changed before she left again for the hospital.

Happy Birthday, Billy Boy

MAMA SETTLES HERSELF in the back seat, twisting her navy pleated skirt like she's smoothing a nest. "If I'd known you were going to be this late," she says, "I could still be fixing my face. I told your daddy to get the camera and come on."

Evanelle doesn't answer. The baby, Billy Buttons, threw up twice and she had to change him skin out, every stitch. Then she had to pick up the cake and flowers. Mama insisted she get silk. "Anything fresh won't last five minutes in that place. They keep it hot as an oven. I took your grandmother an African violet and it didn't live three weeks. *Three weeks!*"

There are roses on the cake. Thirty-six. Evanelle had to wait while they put on every last one of them. And she'd called in her order Friday—decorated. Done everything but spell it. And all the time she ordered, Darren Ravel rubbed her thigh. He kept saying he just *loved* the feel of Arnel. Arnel, her ass. When she told anyone she worked at WKIS, they'd get so excited, their eyes would bulge out and they'd say, "You know D.R. the D.J.?" And she'd say Lord yes, she ought to as long as she worked at KIS. What she didn't say was she knew D.R. more than she wanted to. More than anybody ought to, but that was water over the dam or spilled milk or whatever you wanted to call it.

Billy Buttons sleeps in her arms and Evanelle thinks he is the most beautiful baby in the world. His dark lashes curl up from round cheeks and he sucks air with a pink pucker. He looks stuffed, fat as a frog in his blue terry jumpsuit with anchor buttons and little red sailboats embroidered on the collar. He's growing so fast, no matter what Mama says about bottle babies. It worries Evanelle though when he spits up and that's why she can't say the reason they are late.

Earl pushes in the cigarette lighter, pulls it out again when he remembers he isn't smoking anymore. This is not his idea of a good time. He couldn't have been any slower getting dressed if he tried. Which is another reason they are late. He put on too much musk cologne and Evanelle thinks she may be sick. She feels dizzy, nauseated.

"Let me hold that sweet thing." Mama leans over the front seat, brushes Evanelle's forehead with her stiff hair. Evanelle thinks she feels a red, ugly scratch there. "I never get to hold him," Mama says. "People say I bet you spoil that grandbaby to death, now you finally got one, and I say I don't even have a chance. He's in that awful nursery all the time."

Evanelle would love for Mama to hold the baby. That way if he spit up again Mama would go around the rest of the day smelling soured. "He's asleep," Evanelle says. It almost comes out a sigh.

Mama dangles an earring close to Evanelle's eye and she pulls away from the sharp edges. Mama always said earrings were her weakness. She's got two hundred pair in every color and shape. Drawers of earrings, little trees and cats and birds that hold earrings. When Mama went to get her ears pierced, Evanelle had to hold her hand and it made her feel strange in the middle. There was Billy Buttons kicking her inside . . . only she didn't know it was him then. Earl kept calling him girl names—Tammy Lynn and Loretta Rae and Crystal Sue—all names of his old girlfriends. And Mama kept pulling her on the outside. It gave her a funny feeling she still thinks about sometimes. A feeling that comes back and grabs her from behind like somebody sneaking up when she was little, playing Hide and Go Seek. Sometimes Evanelle feels her life has been turned upside-down like that game they used to play on rainy days in the sixth grade, Fruitbasket Turnover.

Mama folds her rain bonnet. She rattles it like paper and says, "I don't know what on earth can be keeping your daddy." She says this even though she knows Lester Pedy is not Evanelle's daddy; never was, never will be. She just says that to Evanelle to try to make up to her for remarrying and to make her feel more family. "All he had to do was get the camera and close the door. He was right behind me." Mama fans with her folded bonnet. "How long can it take somebody to close a durn door? If he'd been any closer behind, he'd been on my heels and we're late enough as it is." She keeps fanning, making little steam sounds with her breath. "And this rain. I'm proud of Earl for driving."

Earl grunts. Evanelle is proud he's even going. That's all. For over two weeks now, Mama has planned this four-generation thing and Evanelle has worried. Worried about taking Billy in that place. Worried he'll catch something. She doesn't know what, just something. Worried that Earl will act up. He said he didn't see any sense in this business. That it didn't amount to a hill of beans. Evanelle said her family wasn't a hill of beans and she didn't appreciate him talking like that. Then he said that was kinda cute, the way she got mad like she used to and he called her "Pepper Pot" and "Red." He used to say she didn't have red hair for nothing. Actually Evanelle could have hair any color she wanted, but this was one she'd gotten used to and so had everybody else.

Now it covered the gray that was creeping in a hair at a time. At forty-two she saw it coming and she didn't want to be solid white like Mama and going all Easter egg colors; pink, blue, and lavender. Mama had been going to Eunice Platt all her life. Every Friday. And everybody knew Eunice never measured when she mixed. Evanelle had nightmares that she'd be gray-haired in the hospital and the nurses would say things like, "Why honey, this can't be your first!" or ask wasn't she the baby's grandmother? Or giggle behind her back that at her age she should have known better. Well, she couldn't help it. The baby wasn't something she went out and decided. He just happened. Earl acted more surprised than she did. After twenty-two years you just forget, don't expect. She'd never been in love with the idea of kids in the first place and here she was in the middle of this fourth-generation thing, just so Mama could show up her sister Faith Anne who never liked Evanelle from day one. Faith Anne's three daughters had married and divorced and moved twenty states away so they could stay away as much as they liked. So here goes Evanelle, baby and all, to some party in the nursing home. Grandma wouldn't know any of them and Mama would probably hold the baby right up to her face so both of them would have to fight for breath. She accused Evanelle of being peculiar, then taking him to that day nursery where he was exposed to every kind of germ there was. He was in that place so much, Mama said, he wouldn't know anyplace else. Not his real home, nor who his real mama was. It made Evanelle feel like two cents. She didn't work for the fun of it. Lord, she didn't know what they'd live on every week if it wasn't for her paycheck. Earl's didn't seem to go anywhere. She tried to save, but something always came along.

"Where is that man?" Mama rolled down her window. "How long can it take somebody to pull a door shut?" She was ready to yell when Lester backed onto the porch, settled his hat sideways on his head. He had a wide rear like two brown pillows pushed together, a bald doorknob of a head. In some ways Evanelle felt sorry for him; that he lived with Mama seven days a week, twenty-four hours a day. How does he stand it? How do I? How do any of us stand each other? And somehow we'll go on putting up with each other until they put us off in a bed with sides and chairs with wheels to push like Billy Buttons in his stroller.

"Faith Anne has called me fifty times about that cake," Mama says as Lester gets in. "You got it?"

"Right here." Lester pushes the camera in her face.

"I can see that," Mama says, "I'm talking about the cake."

"In the trunk," Evanelle says quietly. What she doesn't say is the cake has only thirty-six roses instead of the eighty-six Mama wanted. Even after Evanelle telephoned the order. She was going to be mad, but it was too late to do anything. Let her be mad, thought Evanelle. I've got this baby and a job and husband to look after. I can't do everything. The baby snored wetly, wiggled like a puppy and snuggled closer. He was sweet even if he did cry a lot and spit up. When he wasn't crying, his face didn't look so puckered and red.

Earl turned at the light and Lester kept clicking the camera, twirled in a roll of film. It snapped like a beetle or something.

"Is that camera what took you so long?" Mama asks.

"I had to find the film," Lester grunts.

"Well, that didn't have to take you all day."

"It wouldn't if you kept things in the place they ought to be." Earl puts the camera to his eye. "I like to never found the film."

"It was in the linen closet the whole time."

Earl hunts a country/western station on the radio to try to drown out the back seat. All he gets is the Radio Gospel Hour and Ministry of the Air. "I've seen the blind learn to see," some preacher yells, "and the lame throw down their crutches and walk. I've seen drunkards lay their bottles down and never reach for them again." Earl turns the radio off.

Evanelle shifts the heavy baby in her arms. It's a wonder all that door-slamming and fuss hasn't waked him up. He makes a snuffling noise and sucks his fist. She hopes that means he's not going to spit up again.

Lester has rolled down his window and Evanelle hears Mama make a noise like she is going to say something about her hair being blown to shreds and changes her mind.

"I sure like this car," Lester says.

"I'll sell her to you." Earl peels off a breath mint, chews. "Nothing down and a hundred when I catch you."

"Har," laughs Lester, "har. I heard tell of deals like that."

Mama pats the back of the front seat. "This is a nice car, Earl. Yours or the company's?"

Mama loves to rub it in that the only car Evanelle has ever owned is the blue one she bought herself when she still lived at home. And Earl has a different one every week, all belonging to the dealer he works for. It's a wonder he hasn't traded or sold Evanelle's, but that's only because she won't let him.

Sometimes Evanelle thinks she's been married a hundred years. Fifty at least. Her life seems to be running away from her and she can't slow it down. It wasn't good having a baby at her age. Not when she'd shut off her mind to the idea a long time ago. Billy Buttons would grow up with a bald daddy and the oldest mama in the first grade while her own mother was going around saying, "I never thought I'd have a grandbaby in the first place and here you go off leaving it with some stranger every day. Nobody could pay me to be away from the only baby I'd ever have when he was at his sweetest and most precious stage."

When Mama says that, Lester always says, "Hush. Now that Nelle's got started, who says she's going to stop. She and Earl may end up with a baseball team yet."

Earl always blushes and grins, says, "I'm all for it." Then he pokes Evanelle in the ribs like he wants her to laugh.

She doesn't see anything to laugh about. Earl slept right through the midnight feedings and on past 5:00 a.m. when

Billy Buttons woke up the day. There wasn't one thing slow about him, even if that's one of the things her doctors worried about at first. Her age. They did the test and everything came back normal. Evanelle knew it would be. Billy Buttons kicked and turned and twisted too much to be the least bit slow.

"If you go slow by here"—Lester leans over the front seat and points for Earl—"right up there. That service station. That's where I found a man with my name once. I tell you that was a crazy feeling."

"I don't know what's crazy about it," Mama snorts. "It's a common name."

"I was selling soap for the car washes and when I walked in that station and saw my name, I like to have backed out. Scared me so." Lester points. "Right there."

The only thing that sits in the spot now is a fruit stand and adult book store. The sign reads "JOY" in big, orange letters. "Tapes, books, records and films."

"It's got so nobody can stay in business anymore," Lester says as they drive past. "Used to be a Gulf station. And the fellow that ran it was honest as they come."

"How you know?" Mama asks. "He buy you out?"

"He didn't buy a thing," Lester says. "But anybody with my same name has got to be an all right fellow."

"Shoot," Mama says. "You're lucky he wasn't a crook. One of the ten most wanted. Picture in the post office. How would you like that?"

"My liking wouldn't have anything to do with it," Lester says. "His face, my name. Now my face in the post office would be a different story. It might just pretty up the place."

"I found my name once." Earl brakes for a light. "In an obituary. Like to have scared me to death."

Then Mama has to tell about the time H.A. (who is Evanelle's real daddy) stopped in a cemetery somewhere in Kansas. "Never been there before nor since—and there was his name big as anything on a tombstone. I tell you if that don't set your mind to thinking, nothing will."

Evanelle has heard the story ten hundred times. She could tell about the time she was scared to death, right recently. When Billy Buttons was born and nobody, nobody was there. Not Earl—he'd gone to Nashville. Not Mama—she'd gone across the river to some outlet store with Gladine Williams and they stopped to look at bedding plants and got to talking and forgot her only daughter in her time of need. Evanelle had called a dozen places from the grocery store to the beauty shop to church and couldn't find one trace of her. Here she was two weeks late and Mama had called every single day for the last month, driving her crazy, asking, "You gone yet?" Then the one day Mama didn't call, Evanelle's water breaks and she has to call a taxi to get to the hospital. She's never been madder nor more embarrassed in her life. Then the driver didn't have change for a twenty and she'd had to stand in front of the hospital and wait—in her condition. Sometimes she didn't know how she got through half the things she did.

They were nearing The Home now. Seven Oaks, but it was only some bent little pines and seven smooth, gray stumps. The oaks had been cut down to add on to The Home and it was too much trouble to change the name. The Home was long and low like a pink motel without a marquee. It had a porte cochere with an ambulance parked under it.

"I called here yesterday," Mama says, "and they're supposed to have her up and dressed. Faith Anne is bringing her an orchid. That's what they told me at the florist. She didn't. Yellow. I said orchids aren't orchids unless they're purple, but it's not me buying. It's her money."

"Florist?" Evanelle shifts the sleeping baby. There is a damp spot on her dress and his hair is plastered down. She tries to fluff it. "I got silk," she says. "That's what you told me."

"I know. I know," Mama says. "But I was by the florist

and just dropped in. You know how Harmon is. If you're within ten miles and don't stop, he gets his feelings hurt."

There are three flags flying in front of Seven Oaks. The state flag, the regular red, white, and blue one, and the other Evanelle can't figure out. It is purple with some sort of yellow trim and design. She can't think what it stands for. Council on Aging? Presidential Seal of Approval? Duncan Hines rating?

Earl eases into a parking place that looks too small. It is an end one and marked off for a small car. "Foreign," says Earl. "I wish they'd outlaw the things. Not let them in the gates of this country."

"I hate to wake him," Evanelle says to nobody in particular.

"Well, if you want to sit in the parking lot all day," Earl says, "we'll let you." He slicks back his hair with both hands, looks in the mirror. When Evanelle was in the eighth grade and Earl was a senior, she fell all over herself trying to make him notice her. He wore duck tails and white loafers and when he did the twist, it was "locomotion." Everybody said they had never seen anybody who could move so much standing in one place. And she'd been a little bitty thing with a ponytail, but he'd noticed. He even said then that she had more up there than most women would have in a lifetime of wishing. Then he went off to the Navy, never wrote once. When he came back, Evanelle was still there, living in the same house, doing the same things, seeing the same people. She worked after school for the radio station, answering the phone, typing spots.

"I hope I never live long enough to have to go to one of these places," Mama says. Earl hands her the flowers, Lester takes the cake, and they leave Evanelle with the baby, diaperbag, and her handbag. She can't figure out how she's going to carry it all, but they have gone up the walk, past an old man in a sea captain's hat sitting in a wheelchair on the porch.

The baby wakes with a wail and Evanelle shifts him to her shoulder, the diaper bag to the other, and somehow grabs her purse. She doesn't have a free hand to shut the car door, so she gives it a boot with her foot and leaves a print on Earl's fresh wash job. She doesn't care. Serves him right.

She's glad it stopped raining or she'd be getting soaked to her toes and the baby too. He turns his eyes to the sky like he sees something, stares.

The old man in the wheelchair holds the door for her with his cane. There is a beach towel spread across his lap that has pictures of punk rockers and the words, "It's a Wild and Crazy World." Evanelle thinks it sure is. Earl and Mama aren't in sight.

"They brought me here and dumped me and haven't been back since," the old man says. He has stubble on his chin like cactus.

"Who?" Evanelle thinks of Earl and Mama.

"My daughter," he says, "and that good-for-nothing she married. That's who."

Evanelle adjusts the baby on her shoulder. Something has fallen from the diaper bag and she drags it behind her like a tail.

"You're losing something," the old man says, pokes at it with his cane.

"I got too much." Evanelle thrusts the baby onto his lap, where the baby begins threshing his legs and cranking up to cry. The old man pokes a stubby brown finger in Billy Buttons's face. "Dooba, booba doo," he says. "This boy won't turn his old daddy out in the world not caring if he lives or dies. Not this boy. No siree."

Evanelle repacks the diapers. Under the wheelchair she notices a lint-ball big and gray as a mouse. Faith Anne has been saying all the time this place wasn't kept clean.

"Yar," the old man says to the baby, who is sucking in air to let out a sharp, red-faced howl. She takes the baby, gives the old man the diaper bag, and he rolls after her. "Some around here," he says, "got chairs that go by themselves. I like to roll my own, thank you."

When they round the corner, Mama and Earl are nowhere to be seen, but Lester is leaning against the wall next to the Coke machine. "Don't tell your mama," he says, draining the last drop. "Air in this place makes my mouth dry."

Evanelle wonders what Coke does to his diabetes. I must look like a parade, she thinks, with the old man in his wheelchair following her, then Lester in the rear. She feels like a drum majorette with her skirt hiked up in front and her thighs showing. Lord, Faith Anne was right, she thinks. This place almost knocks you out with ammonia. It reeks like a giant diaper pail.

There is a crowd of nurses at the nurses' station, pulling at some flowers brought over from a church service. Evanelle thinks the gladolias look rusty and the mums limp and brown-edged. She feels something bump the back of her knees and the old man says, "I didn't go to do it, honey. It's hard to stop when somebody slows down and you got all geared up to go ahead."

The door to her grandmother's room is open and she hears Mama and Faith Anne rattling paper, moving things around. The bed is completely covered with a display of gifts and the cake they've placed at her grandmother's feet. Her grandmother looks small, plastic as a doll in a box, her silver hair screwed in tight wads like French knots. Mama loves to tell everyone The Home has its own beauty shop and everyone gets their hair done once a week whether they want it or not.

Faith Anne and Mama are taking turns posing with Grandma. "Smile, Mama," Faith Anne says. "It won't hurt you."

Grandma flickers her eyes, but keeps the same stony expression.

"Grandma," Evanelle starts.

"Not now, honey," Mama says, cradling Grandma at the

same time she elbows Faith Anne back and smiles for Uncle Frank, who holds the camera. "Hold the thing straight," Mama says. "I don't want you cutting me off. Get both of us in there. Me and Mama."

The baby jumps when the flash goes off, squeezes shut his eyes. He'll probably do that on the picture, Evanelle thinks, but she doesn't care. Lights probably aren't all that good for his eyes anyway. Not so much at one time.

Faith Anne tries to move closer to her mother and sister, but Mama steps in front. "I don't know how many flashes he's got left"—she motions to Frank—"and we want to get the four generations in. That's what we come for."

Faith Anne makes a face and Evanelle thinks if she'd been any younger she would have stuck her tongue out at Mama. Faith Anne looks that peeved.

"I thought it was birthday," Faith Anne says. "That's what it was supposed to be about. I've had four generations three times and nobody made a fuss."

"Well," Mama says, "this is *my* four-generation." She takes the baby from Evanelle, jostles him upright so that he reaches out both arms like someone has a gun in his back. "Look what I brought," Mama shouts to Grandma. "You ever seen anything so cute?" She props him beside the prone woman. "Now Evanelle, honey, you come get on this side and Frank you get us all in the picture and see if you can not make me look as big as you did the last time." Mama jerks Evanelle around close to the bed.

Frank shoots three pictures and each time Evanelle blinks when the flash goes off. She is sure the baby does too. That ought to be next week's winner in the *Horsepoint Herald*. Sometimes they put generation pictures on the front page if nobody robbed a branch bank, there wasn't a flash flood or fire, and nobody shot a deer or killed a big rattlesnake.

"I've waited long enough for my turn." Faith Anne squeezes close between Mama and Evanelle. "I got Mama something she's never had before. A happy birthday card from Ronald Reagan—the President. Look, it's got her name right here." She pushes the card under Mama's nose.

"I can read," Mama says. "It's one like they send to everybody who asks for them."

"You got to be over eighty," Faith Anne says, "and you got to write in months ahead of time. Not everybody in this world gets one."

Evanelle looks at the gold-trimmed card. It does have some signature on it that looks real and it says Ronald Reagan.

"What's she going to do with it?" Mama asks. "I've seen prettier cards before. It's got no design, no color, no flowers, no nothing."

"Nothing but the President's signature," Faith Anne says, and waves the card. "She can put it on her bedside table for all the nurses to see"—she props it behind a water pitcher—"or hang it on the wall." Faith Anne holds the card against the wall, then presses it to her chest. "I just might have it framed for her. Myself."

"You do that," Mama says. "Now move over. We got pictures to take here."

The baby lies like he's been stunned and Grandma reaches one old yellow hand toward him, tries to stroke his hair. She makes a deep noise in her throat that comes out like a bird squeak. Evanelle pushes the baby closer and sits on the edge of the bed.

"We've got to have at least one more picture." Mama motions to Frank. "Let's finish out the roll. Where's Earl?" She goes to the door. "We need Earl. Earl," she calls.

"That's okay," Evanelle says, and takes off her shoe, rubs her foot. "He didn't have anything to do with it." But Mama goes down the hall and comes back pulling Earl, who poses at the head of the bed just like he belongs there, which almost makes Evanelle smile. She knows a secret she'll never tell. Not if she lives to be a hundred. Not if Earl behaves himself like he has lately. Not if D.R. the D.J. goes his merry way and keeps going.

When the pictures come back, Evanelle's eyes aren't closed but she's making a funny mouth and her nose looks like she's been crying. Everybody who sees it in the *Horsepoint Herald* says it's a good picture. After a while Evanelle thinks, "Well, it could've been worse." But she knows different.

The Green Car

IN MY DREAM someone is stealing the car, my old station wagon; its concave side, rusty rear, and temperamental starter. The dogs bark. I stand by the window, watch headlights tarnish clean white moonlight into something tawdry. Two loud men yell to each other like carnival barkers. I can't hear what they say as they slam doors, race the motor; and my car glides down the road smooth as liquid seeking a level.

I watch the scene like something on television. A moment later I get angry. How dare that car start so easily for strangers, when I, its owner, its caretaker and oil-giving friend, have to baby and coax and wheedle it into action, to get it to take me to market and classes, on errands, the girls to school. Where does its loyalty lie?

After anger, there's fright. Why would anyone steal my old car? Are they taking it first and will come back later for more and better things? I see them hauling out my grandmother's silver service, wedding china, the stereo, our TV,

Kate's coin collection. I see them tying my hands, gagging my mouth, so I can't scream rape or whatever I'd scream if there was anyone to hear me.

Most of the time there's no one on this mountain but me. When everyone is home, there are six. Dave and me, the girls, Kate and Chris, and our neighbors, Thad Reeves and his wife, Betts. They live a mile away. Between us we have an assortment of cats, dogs, uncounted wildlife.

The Reeveses have two dogs who visit daily, frolic with our beagles. I know the dogs better than their owners.

We met Thad and Betts once before we moved and I've called her a few times. Mostly at night when she's home from work. She sounded either unfriendly, distant, or bored. I did learn the dogs' names are Red, the setter, and Plasha, the collie.

The dogs' barking wakes me and I'm shaking, but not cold. Dave is snoring steadily when I slide from the bed and stand by the window. Moonlight, pure, unbroken except for the trees, close as pickets, covers everything in a soft snow. It was only a dream. There is no one out there, and my car, worn and wearing the autograph of my city days, stands beside Dave's pickup truck. The dogs bark at deer who touch small feet to trails they knew before we came, built this house, invaded their world.

I know what triggered the dream, what mixture made it. The chilling leftover of yesterday. Another thread knitted into a garment of a shape I refuse to wear. Fear. It fits me like a shadow. I've cleaned and shaken, brushed and put away this garment, mothballed in a closet. But it does belong to me and it hangs there waiting.

I stand by the stove, wait for the fat lady of a teakettle to sound the first note of her scream. Despite the snores, Dave sleeps lightly. He has an eight o'clock lecture class. He was making lesson plans at eleven last night.

After eleven years in the business world, he returned to the university to teach. We left the city and moved to a tiny mountain near a national forest, seventeen miles from the town where the girls go to school, Dave teaches, and I shop. Three days a week, I take a class. "The Progressive Era in America, 1890–1920: Years of Protest and Reform." Someday I'll have my degree.

"You live in paradise," our city friends say. "All this clean air, trees, your own creek, and not a soul for miles, miles." They envy the quiet, the peace of the place, our ferns, wildflowers.

I got a book, tried to identify them, teach the girls. Bloodroot, bleeding-heart, rattlesnake plantain. Our woods are full of birds. I try to learn their names and calls. Of ones I can't identify, Dave says, "Name them yourself. Call them anything you want. Red bird, blue bird, brown bird."

I hear birds now; a cardinal flies to the feeder as I make coffee.

With my steaming cup I wind through the house, in and out of rooms, touch things. The girls in blanket cocoons, polished tabletops, moist soil around plants.

The prayer plant in the living room has its leaves closed tight for the night. I never see it closing, or opening, but only fully awake and asleep. I sleep only to dream the bad dreams, the dark residue of yesterday.

Yet I like the soft hours before dawn, the silence of the sleeping house, the even breathing of the furnace, the way early light slants through the trees.

I feel in command, mistress of the manor with my family in tow. It's only after Dave leaves, the girls are gone, that I am afraid. Can I make it alone?

At the market in town, when I cash checks and clerks read my address they ask, "Aren't you afraid out there?"

Before yesterday I had given a negative answer. Said, what was there to fear? The quiet was so nice, the woods and creek beautiful; the feeling of owning all the mountain, acres, acres of it.

Someday there will be other houses here. The town will

grow, land sell, other people build.

"It will never be a gossip-over-the-back-fence–type place," Dave said. "No houses close enough to smell back yard grills."

People who choose to live out here have an independence about them, Dave said. Like us, I thought, like the Reeveses.

I hadn't recognized Betts's voice last night when she phoned, only that she was someone upset. She wanted to know if I had seen anything unusual, any strange cars? Strange men?

Nothing. I had been to class, the library, picked up the girls at school, then home.

The Reeveses' house was broken into, Betts said. A few things taken. Nothing valuable, a rifle, some money and food, but she was upset.

My first thought was that it could have been our house. That I could have been home when the thieves came. Alone.

"What could I do?" I asked Dave.

"Simply say, 'I have a gun and if you take one more step, I'll blow your head off.'"

"But I don't have a gun," I said. Dave has talked for weeks about buying a gun. I refuse. Feel it is more dangerous to have a gun around the house. Home accidents, the girls. I would worry so much with a gun in the house.

"That person out there"—Dave pointed toward the door—"won't know whether you have a gun or not. Living out like this, he might well assume you do."

But instead I am the pioneer wife, at home alone, protecting the homestead . . . with empty arms. I think of all the women on *Gunsmoke* and inside my head I practice my line. Take one more step, Mister, and I'll blow your head off. I can't convince even myself. My voice sounds thin, silly, and anything but fierce. Even the dogs don't listen to me.

These city dogs. They go partway with me to the mailbox, sniff, take small side trips, hit a fresh deer track, and are off for half the day. None of my calls brings them back or keeps them home. At those times I feel deserted. The dogs are not really protectors. They would melt under a stranger's touch. But I bank on the fact that most strangers wouldn't know that. They do bark convincingly at times, growl to protect the bones of dead deer they bring up. Our woods are posted against hunters, but they come anyway. I often hear shots, sometimes very close, and I worry the dogs, or I, might be mistaken for deer.

I check the dogs' bed outside. It's empty. They are off even now, chasing the deer they saw earlier. The barks that woke me.

The mist through the trees is lovely and I like the smell of early morning, dew-damp woods. I take several deep breaths and go wake the girls.

"Your face is cold." They snuggle deeper into their blankets.

Dave's electric razor is going and by the time he is showered and dressed I have bacon on plates, an omelet in the oven.

"What's the occasion?" He pours coffee.

"Two more days until Saturday." I take the tongues of toast from the toaster.

Kate fusses, "Isn't there any jam but grape?"

Dave tells her to eat grape or plain, or not at all, but they do have to hurry. An early class means he takes the girls and I am spared the struggle with the car. I won't have to hear the usual gripes from the back seat as I jiggle and coax the old car to life.

"Why don't we get a new car?" Kate said last week.

"Because this is a good car," I said.

"If it's a good car, why won't it start?" Chris sat, fat in her overcoat, hair streaming down her back like ribbons.

"Because it needs something fixed." Dave has said one of the guys in Vocational at school can fix it. Why take it to a garage and spend forty or fifty bucks when Frank says he'll do it for free?

"When?" I asked.

"When he gets around to it," Dave said. "One of these days."

I get so tired of waiting for one of these days.

"You're hurting the economy," Chris said one morning. "When people like us don't buy new cars, it puts other people out of work."

"If people like us buy new cars when they can't afford them, then we hurt our economy."

"We have the truck," Kate said quietly, books on her lap.

Kate, the practical. "Yes, we do, don't we?" I laugh. "And the truck starts." It roars at a touch, leaps like a huge wild horse. Scares me. I need a mounting block to get into it.

Dave loves to drive the truck, gets teased at school. I drive it reluctantly. It isn't me. I'm not the size or temperament, not the self-sufficient farmer's wife. When I shop, the groceries sit beside me on the seat like brown bagged people.

"Is everyone ready?" Dave grabs his briefcase, gives me a gritty toothpaste kiss.

"Take the car today. Leave me the truck."

"I didn't think you liked the truck." Dave looks puzzled.

"I don't. It's just that . . ."

"What?"

"If the truck is here . . . I mean, if there's a truck parked in the drive, they might think a man is home."

"Who might think a man is home?"

"Whoever broke into the Reeveses' house yesterday."

"Why do you think they'll come back?" He tries to read my eyes, looks long enough to see down to my toes.

"Don't you?"

"No, I really don't. What did they take? Food, some loose change, a gun. They weren't pros. I think it was kids hitchhiking, taking a trail through the woods."

I think they could still be here, hiding. Waiting. "Betts was quite upset."

"And her hysteria rubbed off on you, right?"

I swallow a lump of cold coffee. "Not really, but what if—?"

"They won't." He sounds positive. "Most break-ins happen during the day when no one is home." He checks the door locks, gives me a kiss. "Make sure the doors are locked."

Last week I had come home from class to find the door open, living room full of leaves, and a dog asleep in each chair. I was frightened and went through the house checking closets, under beds, behind shower doors, and even then could not relax until Dave and the girls got home.

The door had simply blown open. It had not been shut tightly. But I asked myself, what would I have done had I found someone? I don't know.

I scrape dishes, load the dishwasher, look up to see a shadow flick past my window. My imagination. The first week we lived here, I saw someone outside my kitchen window and was near a scream, when he lifted his cap, said, "I'm from the electric company, ma'am. Here to check the meter." There had not been a single bark from the dogs. They had been off for a swim in the lake, hunting a delicious scent, leaping after a deer. No loyalty—like the car.

"Sandy," Pete calls from the drive, "I can't get the car started. And if I keep working on it, I'll be late. Sorry."

I wave from the deck until the truck disappears—stand there until I no longer hear the motor, only birds and trees and my own breathing. I go back to the dishes, routine things.

While the vacuum runs, I try to organize my term paper. Number my notes, footnotes.

When I glance up and out the window I see a green car slowly going past our road. It almost stops, then goes on.

At first I'm frightened; then I relax. A lot of times people take a wrong turn off the highway and often there are inquiries about buying property, since most of it is still unsold.

The car comes back, turns in our drive, stops. Two men

get out. One is a boy in jeans. His boots crunch across the gravel as he walks to my car and gets in. *He gets in my car.* This is last night's dream, but real. It's happening and I don't know what to do. The other man comes toward the house.

The car starts and goes halfway down the drive before it stops, idles.

I run to the phone, find the number I typed on a card taped to the base. 983–111 . . . large black type. My fingers are wet and slip as I dial. Hurry, hurry, hurry. The sheriff will know where to come. He was at the Reeveses' yesterday.

Someone knocks on my door. Do thieves knock? Is it a guise? Should I say nothing, wait for them to break in?

"Mrs. Paxton," he calls.

I still don't answer. He could have read our name off the mailbox. The phone is ringing at the sheriff's office. Once, twice, three times. Where are they? Why don't they answer?

"Pete sent us to get the car."

I hang up the phone.

"It's Frank Willis from Vocational, over at school," he says. "Pete told me a few weeks ago he wanted me to take a look at the car. He reminded me a while ago."

I remember Frank from the faculty picnic—thin, dark-haired, glasses, very unlike my idea of a mechanic.

"Pete gave me his keys and I brought one of the students to drive it in." Frank stands on the deck, smiles. "I thought I better tell you, so you wouldn't think we were stealing it." He laughs.

"Thank you." I can't laugh, or even attempt any sort of a smile. "You did scare me."

"Gosh." He waves his arms. "This is a great place to live. Don't you love it?" He reaches down to scratch the ears of one of the dogs who have come from the woods, sit thumping, smiling at his feet.

I glare at the dog. Where were you when I needed you?

Frank waves, goes back to the green car. "See you later."

The dogs run, circle around me, jump for attention. "Why

don't you stay home?" I ask them. They only thump and smile, fenced city dogs relishing in their new freedom. They want to explore coves, creeks, follow every trail.

I go into the house for my red jacket, slip it on, tucking my hair into the knitted red hood. Keys in my pocket, I carefully lock the doors and head toward the mailbox. The dogs rush past, look back as if to say, come on, let's run. Sometimes I do run and laugh and look at my shadow like a child. I whoop and call hello to hear my voice, to know that I am not afraid.

I walk between trees, over the bridge. The creek rushes around the rocks, charges and roars like a tan beast. At places it rises up full of challenge and spunk.

I take a deep cool breath, then hum as I walk up the road, hands deep in my pockets. I've never learned to whistle. This is a good time to try.

Rules and Secrets

MISS MELODY MCLEAN was from Virginia. No one knew how she came to teach that one year in a small town in the North Carolina mountains, but there she was the first day of school, sitting on her desk, rollbook in hand, checking us off as if we were a shipment of rare goods she had waited a long time for. Her red-orange hair waved and curled with a mind of its own and her green eyes always saw something to smile about. She wore a plaid skirt, white organdy blouse, green vest, and swung her long freckled legs. She had more freckles than anyone I'd ever seen. Arms, legs, face—more freckles even than Vaden Stringer, who had a million. One time Miss McLean hugged Vaden and said, "If there was a freckle-counting contest, Vaden and I would tie for first place." He smiled wider than anyone had ever seen him. Maybe because nobody had hugged him before. Most of the teachers tried to stay as far away from him as possible and nobody wanted to be the one in front of or directly behind him in line. He usually smelled. Like car motors or oil or grease.

His father ran the local garage, the family lived above it, and Vaden must have played in and around the grease pits. Teachers gave up long ago when they inspected nails. Vaden was always passed over. Except by Miss McLean. Vaden began to come to school with cleaner shirts, sometimes ironed and free of grease spots, and he started combing his hair. He worked on his hands and they were cleaner. Not as clean as anybody else's hands, but wonderfully clean for Vaden.

Miss McLean always noticed when anyone wore anything new—scarf, blouse, shirt, jeans, sweater, socks—and commented. "That's a pretty new dress, Lucy," she'd say. Lucy Estridge looked down to see what dress she was wearing and said, "It's just one my mother made."

"How wonderful to have such a talented mother." Miss McLean touched the collar. "Not everyone can sew and it means you can have so many more clothes."

Lucy looked like she'd never thought about it like that before. And began to say when she had something new, before anyone could comment, "My mother made me this dress." Or blouse, or skirt. Her mother even made Lucy a coat and jumper of soft green wool. We envied Lucy now and wished our mothers could sew.

Lucy was pretty that year. Maybe she always was and we'd never really looked at her before. The way no one had ever listened to Carolyn sing. We didn't know she could sing until Miss McLean picked her for the part of Dinah Shore for the Friday assembly. And Kenny Stone. "Crooner," we called him for weeks afterward, and he looked it. All the fifth-grade girls got his autograph and used to follow him on the playground. Skinny Kenny Stone with the thick glasses and pointed nose. Miss McLean took the glasses off, combed his hair back like Bing Crosby, and put him behind the broomstick microphone. He had a wonderful, deep voice. There was swooning in assembly that Friday. Carolyn wore her older sister's pink satin evening gown with the sweetheart neckline and borrowed her grandmother's fox fur piece. She was glamorous, she was Hollywood, after Miss McLean made her up, swept back her hair on one side, and pinned in a silk carnation. Bing—er—Kenny was clear and strong. The rest of the year Carolyn and I sang as we walked home from school.

But Miss McLean wasn't all play and music. She said a lot, "Work when you work, play when you play." We worked when we worked. But it was fun. Arithmetic problems became real when she substituted our names for the ones in the book, or the names of businesses in town. History was acted out—if you read your assignment and knew what to do. Spelling was always two teams chosen for six weeks at a time, with the winners receiving certificates Miss McLean made. She had two shelves of her own books, brought from home, for us to read, check out, and take home. We'd read all the good ones in the library and I loved books with her name in them in that fancy, curling handwriting.

"I don't know what that teacher's doing," Mama said one night, "but your math grades are improving. She's got you really interested and working like you should for the first time."

Miss McLean had us working in partners. We switched every week, graded each other's papers and studied together. It was fun every week but the one I had with Sylvia Hurley. She cried when you marked one of her answers wrong, begged you not to. How was she going to learn if you didn't mark wrong answers? And she missed a lot of them. She copied over every paper and put in the right answers. I had to mark 100 on it so she could show her mother.

Sylvia was the only one unhappy that year. She'd always come to school looking like she'd been crying. Sometimes there were bruise marks on her arms or legs. She was last in line to everything and nobody wanted her on their team for softball. Most of the time she wouldn't play anyway, but sat on the bank by herself and didn't even watch. If the ground was damp, Miss McLean spread her jacket or sweater for Sylvia to sit on. That was one of the few times Sylvia smiled, looked even a little happy.

We were on the playground the day Sylvia's mother came to school and argued at Miss McLean. We couldn't hear everything she said, but she kept jerking Sylvia by the collar of her dress, pulling her arms, and Sylvia cried. "My child wouldn't steal your handkerchief," Mrs. Hurley yelled. "She's not a thief."

"Of course not," Miss McLean said. "Nobody ever thought she was."

Mrs. Hurley yelled some more things that didn't make sense and Miss McLean kept saying, "I *gave* Sylvia my handkerchief. She had a cold and didn't have one."

That seemed to make Mrs. Hurley even more angry and she started yelling a lot of things about taking care of her own child's needs and Miss McLean kept saying she knew she did and Sylvia was such a well-behaved student, tried so very hard in every subject and so on. Miss McLean's voice was sweet and nice. Once she reached to put her arm around Sylvia but Mrs. Hurley jerked her away. Finally, more upset than ever, yelling and screaming things, she grabbed Sylvia's elbow and pulled her away. We watched them walk off the playground. When we grouped around Miss McLean to return to class, tears had dried on her cheeks and she excused herself to stop by the teacher's lounge.

Nobody could understand what the fuss had been about. Of course Miss McLean had given Sylvia the handkerchief. She was always doing things like that, loaning her books, pencils . . . to all of us. Whatever we needed. And when we finished, we returned them. Sylvia must have kept the handkerchief, wanted it, because Miss McLean was so special, and everything that belonged to her was special. Her handkerchiefs had monograms in the corners and were trimmed with lace. Miss McLean wouldn't have cared if Sylvia had stolen the handkerchief. She would have let her keep it, if she'd ask. What was one handkerchief? Who would steal one? Who would accuse anyone of stealing something so silly? Something at all. Not Miss McLean. But why did she cry?

We were all in our seats and strangely quiet when Miss McLean, face washed and lipstick freshened, came in. She still looked pale, moved some books and papers to sit on the corner of her desk. "I wish that you had not had to witness the incident on the playground a few minutes ago. And I hope you won't feel or act any differently toward Sylvia because of it. Except to be more understanding with her and toward her. She can't change the way things are in her life, not yet—maybe not ever—and we can help by being more patient, less critical. We won't mention this again." She picked up the geography book, turned to the chapter on "African States," pulled down the pink and green map, got down to business.

On the way home Carolyn and I talked. Last year, other years, Sylvia had been called "Bird Legs" or "Bird Brain" or "Feather Face"—ugly names—and she'd shrugged them off, even smiled. I was glad we'd never called her things, but I remembered times I'd giggled when somebody else did, and felt terrible. Times when I got to choose teams and waited until last to pick her, hoping the other captain would, then yelled at her when she dropped a fly ball on the third out and we lost.

Carolyn and I invited Sylvia to the church Halloween party, offered to give her a ride. At five-thirty she called, said her mother was going out and she had to go with her. Sylvia sounded like she'd been crying.

"I'd cry too," Carolyn said, "if my mother made me miss the Halloween party."

Lights were on at Sylvia's house, the car in the drive, when we drove past at nine, taking Benny Cushman home. "I bet she didn't go out at all," Carolyn said. We didn't mention it to Sylvia—the party or anything. Some things are better left unsaid, Miss McLean had said a long time before about anger and retaliation. We liked the sound of that word, new words, but she didn't write it on the board as she usually did any new word we heard or asked about.

Anger was like a shade pulled over her face the day she read aloud—according to instructions—the new school policy toward Christmas, against gifts and "any said and possibly planned parties" at school. This was the word sent down from the superintendent's office. The law of the red brick land. "No student shall give any teacher a Christmas present. Due to the differences in circumstances, since all students are not able to give gifts of equal value, none shall be given. And consequently, no teacher shall give students gifts of any kind. There will be no Christmas parties allowed in any classroom in the system. To facilitate janitorial and maintenance services, holiday decorations should be kept to a minimum." Miss McLean's face got darker and darker as she read the notice. We didn't understand it. In the past, I'd given teachers gifts, small gift-wrapped boxes with the bow the biggest thing about them. Usually earrings, lotion or perfumed soap, a scarf. Carolyn and I spent hours in the dime store picking out the perfect gift for our teachers. The day we left school for our holidays was always party day. With cupcakes and punch, games (how many words can you make out of the words "Merry Christmas"?) and carols, listening to the *Nutcracker Suite* or a teacher reading Dickens's "Christmas Carol." We could have none of that this year? It wouldn't be Christmas. Who was the superintendent of schools? Scrooge? There were cries of protest around the room, *Oh no*'s and *How could anyone be so mean?* At Christmastime? It was awful.

Miss McLean thought so too, but she didn't say much. "In Virginia, I gave my class a party. I was planning—"

She was going to give us a party? No teacher had ever done that before. Room mothers came in and gave parties with cupcakes and candy canes, Santa napkins, but a teacher giving her class a party was something else. "Please, Miss McLean," we begged, "isn't there any way we can still have the party? We won't invite the superintendent. We won't tell the principal. We'll be so quiet no one will know."

She grinned with a small shake of her head. "I wish I could."

"Why can't you?" Kenny Stone stood at his desk. "No one would have to know. We can keep it a secret."

Miss McLean laughed, looked at us in a warm, sad way. "Oh my little dears . . . it would never work."

"And if she went against the rules, she'd be fired," said Bruce Stern. His daddy was a deputy for the sheriff's department, wore a uniform with a badge, carried a gun. Sometimes he picked Bruce up at school in the county car. "Using taxpayers' gas," Daddy said. "I don't think it's right." But he did it anyway and nobody said anything.

Miss McLean's giving the class a party herself was not using taxpayers' money, nor school funds. Why couldn't she do it? Carolyn and I discussed it walking home. Life was unfair, school was unfair, and whoever was superintendent wanted to make Christmas miserable for us.

The next day, Miss McLean asked everyone to stay for a few minutes after final bell. We would have stayed forever for her.

"This class *is* going to have a Christmas party," she announced, her eyes sparkling.

We looked at each other, mouthed *oh boy, oh boy*. Then remembered. "How?" asked Carolyn. "The rule made by the superintendent. You'll—"

"Maybe not," Miss McLean smiled. "I'll have the party at my apartment, on my own time, and that shouldn't get anybody in trouble." She wrote the time on the board. An open house, six until eight o'clock, and her address.

She never told us not to tell. Somehow we knew. We were breaking a rule and keeping a secret about it. That made the party even more special, exciting. But what to tell our parents?

I solved that by spending the night with Carolyn. We did that on Friday nights often. And we simply told Carolyn's mother we were going to an open house at Miss McLean's.

Carolyn wore her blue velvet dress with lace collar and cuffs, her new coat with the white rabbit collar, and both of us wore our Sunday slippers, white ankle socks and matching charm bracelets we exchanged for Christmas, opening them early to wear to the party.

The streets had been scraped dry of snow that frosted yards, shrubbery, and rooftops and made the world look like a Christmas card. Chimneys ballooned out plumes of smoke and we stopped every block or so to admire our bracelets or try to puff out a perfect ring of breath.

Miss McLean had a wreath of fresh balsam on her door with holly, pine cones, and a soft red bow. Christmas music and the smell of something hot, orange, and spicy met us at the door, opened by Kenny Stone, in sport coat and tie. Sylvia took our coats, hung them in the closet.

Miss McLean, with a moss-green bow in her hair, matching long skirt and red gingham blouse, poured punch, gave us small sandwiches and decorated cookies.

We stood around like strangers. Everyone looked so dressed up and so pretty—even Sylvia. I wondered what she'd told her mother, and if she came alone? Probably Miss McLean would take her home, though none of us lived more than six blocks or so from school.

I'd walked by this apartment building every school day for six years and had never seen inside. Four teachers lived in four apartments. Sometimes we saw wash on the line and guessed what belonged to who. Sometimes we giggled when we recognized a blouse or shirtwaist dress of the second-grade teacher or Miss Beal, the librarian.

The living room had bookshelves on each side of the fire-place that reached the ceiling, all painted white, as were the walls; green wool carpet, matching drapes, and an armchair of the same color. There was a small desk by the window, a yellow lamp with a shade of different kinds of birds. I decided Miss McLean graded homework papers there. Unless she used the kitchen table, my favorite place at home rather than the kneehole desk in my bedroom. There was a mirror above the fireplace and I looked at all of us framed there, the lights, laughter, and Miss McLean lifting red punch from a crystal bowl, candles reflecting in her cheeks, her eyes. Sylvia, by the door, important, collecting coats, placing them carefully on hangers. And Kenny Stone by the fireplace, Bruce Stern putting on another log.

Later we sang carols around the piano, Miss McLean playing softly, as she sometimes did on rainy days when we could get the music room off the auditorium. Carolyn sang "Silent Night" as a solo, then "O Little Town of Bethlehem" as a duet with Bruce. Everyone sang "We Three Kings" last and as we left Miss McLean gave us gifts—two new red pencils apiece, saying, "I don't want to hear anyone say they don't have a pencil next time I announce a spelling test."

We laughed, gave mock groans. Then she gave us each an envelope with our names written in red ink, said, "Merry Christmas."

Carolyn and I didn't open the envelopes until we were outside. Under the streetlights we dug from the envelope three movie passes, "Admit One" to the Center Theater. We hugged each other, dancing in the cold. Movies! Three free passes. Nothing could have been as wonderful. She was giving us the world for three Saturday afternoons: Tom Mix, Superman, Wonder Woman, Roy Rogers and Dale Evans, Lash LaRue . . . the Pan-a-View News, popcorn and Cokes. Each other. No teacher had ever given us a party before, certainly not at her home, with gifts. Pencils, because she was serious about school and leaning and wanted us to be too. Movie passes because she believed life should have some fun in it.

Fun was movies on Saturdays, but it was also school five days a week. I denied colds, sore throats, and low fevers that year, to keep my mother from keeping me home. Missing a day would have meant missing everything, seeing everybody, Miss McLean. Almost nobody was absent, even Sylvia, who last year had been on the absent list several days a week, looked bluish, pale, and thin shivering in her chair when she was there. She moved that spring, an oddity for the town and our lives. Each year we had the same people, from first grade on. You knew who you wanted to sit beside, be on your relay, dodgeball, softball team. Sylvia didn't say goodbye. No one knew until the Monday morning Miss McLean, with a firm mouth, made the announcement and started the day's work. We wondered where she moved? Why would anyone move before school was out? And especially since we were planning a May Day. Lucy's mother was making costumes, Carolyn's blue and mine yellow. A long dress with the skirt a complete circle. We couldn't wait.

My father grumbled behind his newspaper that he was "paying good money for a dress that will only be worn once. Somebody in this town has big ideas."

A seventh-grade girl, Sarah Grambling, was May Queen. She was beautiful, blond with round blue eyes, the longest dark lashes in the world, and a different angora sweater for each day of the week.

Three of us were chosen for the May Court. We were to wear lacy picture hats, carry bouquets of real daisies. Daddy said it was too much for a little elementary school in a small town.

Mother said it was going to be beautiful and she hoped he could get off work to come.

He didn't answer.

Mother kept rolling my hair on leather curlers, twisting them tight to my head. "I try," she sighed, "even if it doesn't stay in."

I thought of Miss McLean who never had to roll her hair at all, how it waved, curled, and did things by itself. Like she did. All energy and sparkle and fun. She suggested the May

Day, planned and directed it. And it was beautiful, more beautiful than even my mother thought.

The whole town turned out to see the king and queen crowned, the throne Miss McLean borrowed from one of the churches set atop a platform covered with red felt. There was a red runner on the front lawn and a processional for the presentation of the court. I bobbed and bowed, didn't spill flowers from my basket. Court jesters did card tricks and juggled. Toby Simpson rode his unicycle and Kenny Stone's black and white dog did tricks.

Fathers took pictures, some movies of it all. The Maypoles were braided to music, unbraided, then woven again. Everyone said it was beautiful, and parents kept repeating this to the principal, superintendent, who stood stiff and out of place in dark suits, narrow ties. They didn't smile much, complained about the heat "so early in the year," and brushed playground dust from their polished shoes.

Summer vacation and the end of the school year came too fast. The last day nobody wanted to leave. We stayed to stack books, rewash boards, put chairs on tables, take down decorations, divide up the plants, discard dead science projects, and clean out closets. Anything to linger. Miss McLean shushed us when we said there would never be another teacher we'd love as much as her, another year that would be more fun. "Go on with all of you." She headed us toward the door. "Get on with the business of growing up." She hugged everybody, touseled Bruce Stern's hair and told Carolyn to keep singing.

What was she going to do this summer? "Going back to Virginia," she said.

"See you next year," we called, feeling lightheaded to leave the classroom without an armload of books, homework assignments.

The next week Carolyn and I went to her apartment to visit. We promised ourselves we wouldn't go in—or maybe only for a glass of iced tea—if she invited us. For an excuse we carried potholders we'd woven on a lap loom Carolyn got for her birthday.

There was no answer at the door. We heard it ring when we rang again. It was working. Surely she hadn't packed and left so soon. Not for the whole summer. We weren't tall enough to peer in the door glass, so we had to find a low window, one that looked in the living room. The empty, empty living room. And kitchen and bedroom.

We couldn't believe it. "Maybe she found a better apartment," Carolyn said.

"In this town?" It wasn't possible.

Or moved to a house? My daddy would have said something. He sold real estate—but not lately. I heard him tell people, "I *used* to sell real estate."

She had moved. Disappeared, left our lives. We would never see her again. Carolyn and I said it must have been Sylvia who told. Or Sylvia's mother.

Bruce Stern said once at the swimming pool he had gotten a letter from Miss McLean. But he never showed it to anyone and he liked to tell lies.

Who Cooks for You?

WHEN BONNIE ROSE set out with her basket and tester, she always felt a little like Red Riding Hood. She went over highways and past woods, to country homes and city apartments. She was your handy-dandy microwave demonstrator "by appointment only." It wasn't a bad job for part-time. She made her own schedule juggling appointments between other people's hours and her classes and family. It wasn't easy, but she liked most of the people she had met, and she usually outran the wolves. Since her husband, Pete, lost his job eighteen months before, the wolves always seemed to be after her: the food market wolf, the mortgage wolf, the utility company wolf, the charge account wolf. They snapped at her heels, threatened, nipped and snarled. She felt their hot breath on her neck, heard them groan in her sleep, but she kept them away tossing tidbits.

Today's wolf was real. He had glittering eyes, a neat little beard, two steaks and a chilled bottle of wine. She walked right into his parlor with her basket and job. How could she not have known?

21C Brakston Court was a brick duplex with peeling trim and torn black shutters. Bonnie Rose checked her notebook as she rang the bell. Yunger, Fredrick. The space beside Wife's name was empty, but sometimes the company sales- person simply failed to fill it in. The shrubbery beside the porch was shaggy and behind it were beer cans, an upended pizza box. She's been in this demonstration business for a year now and in all kinds of houses, met all kinds of people. The ones who apologized for their "mess" were usually the ones with a spotless house, a kitchen that looked like a floor covering ad in magazines. They waxed and polished even drawer pulls. She loved those kitchens. In others she smiled and started with how to keep their microwave ovens clean: glass tray, interior walls, the door.

"Mr. Yunger?" Bonnie Rose saw a maroon terry jogging suit unzipped to his waist, dark curly chest hair, and lizard-skin cowboy boots. "Is Mrs. Yunger home?"

"I'm it," he laughed. "Come in. The oven's in the kitchen like a good little oven should be. Or do you want it some other place? I can move it for a lady's convenience." He smiled, held the door.

"Wine?" he asked, and poured a glass.

"No, thank you—I'm really on a very tight schedule. I need an ice cube, though."

"In your wine? You like it iced? It's more bodied at room temperature. If you've never tried it—"

"An ice cube for the demonstration," she said firmly be- tween her teeth, and reached inside the freezer, past a decal on the refrigerator door of a huge pink panther holding a glass of champagne.

"Here, let me." He brushed against her. "Oops, sorry."

She didn't know if he was making a pass, extremely clumsy, slightly drunk, or all three. All she knew was she wanted to get her demonstration done and get out of there fast.

"This is your program for defrosting," she said, but he didn't seem to be listening. He poked in a drawer. "You smoke?" he said.

"No," she said. Her head felt wooden. She could go through her talk in her sleep, like a nursery rhyme . . . And this is how we thaw our food so quickly in the evening. Her feet ached. Her throat felt scratchy.

"For temperature-controlled cooking," she continued, "use your probe."

"So that's what the little devil is." He twirled the probe in his fingers. "Well, I'll be probed and prodded and—"

"In this mode"—she inserted the probe—"you can program the temperature and it will hold indefinitely."

"That's me," he said. "On hold indefinitely unless you can do something about it." He moved around the counter, reached toward her. "Look, honey—"

She stepped back. Her elbow hit the wine glass, knocked it over. She grabbed her basket and ran. She probably left the door open, churned and spun gravel in his driveway getting away so fast. She didn't care. All she knew was to get out as fast as she could. She remembered his open mouth as she ran. She should have shoved the oven in it.

Still shaking, she screeched to a stop at a traffic light. The nerve of the Hairy Little Bastard. She'd heard other demonstrators talk of HLBs at their monthly meetings. Several had bachelors or newly divorced guys make suggestive remarks about flanks and being well-done. "Everybody gets at least one," her supervisor had said. But Bonnie Rose had never had one until today. Well, they can have it, she thought, and this job too. She wanted to pound her dash, sit on her horn, kick and scream and yell. Something. She looked in her mirror. What if he followed her? But a blue sedan was behind, a man who looked tired, distracted. Beside her, a station wagon with two blond toddlers batting balloons. She glanced down and saw she was still wearing her red "Deluxe Foods" apron. She laughed and kept laughing. Anyone seeing her would have thought she was some runaway housewife. People in the cars around her probably thought she was some mad woman. She *was* mad—angry, angry, angry. Bonnie Rose pressed the accelerator; the car surged forward.

There was an ache between her shoulders. When she pulled in at home she noticed Pete's truck parked at an odd angle, the tailgate down.

She heard hammering as she put her books on the hall table. What was Pete doing? She followed the hammering to Marty's bedroom, where everything from the closet lay heaped on the bed—toys, clothes, shoes. Pete was putting shelves in Marty's closet. The organizing shelves she'd mentioned months, maybe two years before. Pete poked his head out, grinned. "Hi, babe."

"It's going to be neat, huh, Mom?" Marty said.

"Great, but what about Scouts?" Bonnie Rose looked at the shavings, sawdust, scattered tools. "And what about dinner?"

"Do I have to go?" Marty said. He picked up a baseball mitt, kneaded it. "I'd rather help Dad."

"It's okay by me," Bonnie Rose said, "but what about your derby entry and money for the campout? It's due tonight."

"I guess I'd better go." Marty laid the glove down.

"Hey," Pete said somewhere from the closet, "I guess I forgot."

He also forgot dinner. She'd left instructions on the refrigerator door to thaw the ground beef and make the Chili Casserole.

She didn't say it was okay, because it wasn't.

Breakfast was still on the table. Cereal, sugar, coffee cups. God, she hated a dirty kitchen, and she wasn't going to cook in one when she wasn't being paid to do it.

She checked the schedule. Lucy's turn. So where was Lucy? In the library. Lucy had scribbled a note on the telephone pad. Thanks a lot, Bonnie Rose thought. Other people around here have to study too.

I won't touch it, she thought. I won't touch a thing if it's midnight when she gets home. Someone around here has to teach responsibility.

Bonnie Rose picked up her textbook, went to the porch. She was glad she made good notes. Now all she had to do was carve out time to really go over them, to concentrate. She couldn't do it! She was tired, hungry, upset, harried, and at the bottom of the well. Pete had been out of work a year and a half now. His company had relocated and was consumed by a merger, and the parent company had someone on staff for his job. Cost Accounting. He was good at it, but there wasn't a vacancy within two hundred miles. They could move, but not for another six months. She had one more semester to get her teacher's certificate. "Wherever we are there will always be schools, and schools have to have teachers. Teaching is a job and that way at least one of us will have a job." She'd been back in school almost a semester and she both loved and hated it. She loved the fact that the classroom and her assignments took her mind off money worries. She liked her classes. She liked looking at learning and how it worked, why certain methods were appropriate to certain types of learners, but she hated the way her life was scheduled down to minutes. Even sleep was a luxury.

Beside Pete's chair was his coffee cup, an overflowing ash tray. He could at least pick up around here. Mail lay on the floor. Most of the time the people Pete contacted through the classified ads never bothered to reply. She flipped through circulars, envelopes addressed "Occupant," a dentist's bill, utility statement—$89.75, and that was not even using the dryer. It was broken. The last letter had the Deluxe Foods logo. Bonnie Rose's hand shook. More demos. She couldn't. She just wouldn't—not after today. She was still so angry she wanted to bite something very hard and scream very loudly. Damn, damn, damn.

"Hon." Someone touched her shoulder and Bonnie Rose jumped. "Don't. Don't." She started crying, shaking.

"What's wrong?" Pete said. "What's wrong?"

"Don't touch me."

"I only wanted to say Scouts meet in twenty minutes and I can stop by for burgers on the way back."

She didn't answer, but rushed past him to the bathroom, where she cried into a towel until her cheeks felt raw. Pete rubbed her back, hugged her. "Whatever it is, it isn't worth it." He rocked her. "You do too much. You don't have to make Dean's List. You don't have to be the best Deluxe Foods demonstrator. You push yourself too hard."

"And you're not pushing at all," she screamed. "You charged more lumber and the account is past due now and—and—"

"I'm taking Marty to Scouts." His mouth was a hard, dark line. "Then we'll talk."

When he came back she had washed her face, put on fresh lipstick, and made a cup of lemon tea. She told him about the latest wolf.

Pete's face flamed. "Who the hell does he think he is? Who do you report this to?"

"No one, really." She shook her head. "And nothing happened except he tried. I don't have to go back there."

"But what about the next one?"

"I can handle it."

"Why don't you quit? Tell Deluxe they can have this great job."

"I'd love to, but it's three hundred dollars a month that's paying some bills and it's something I can schedule in with my classes. We have to think about that."

"It doesn't pay enough for that kind of harassment. You don't have to do it."

"I don't want to do it. I don't want to ever go through my song-and-dance-and-this-is-how-to-cook-your-food-so-fast—"

"There's got to be other things." He let go her hands, walked to the window. "I'd like to do small jobs for people . . . home contracting, repairs . . . little things the big companies don't have time to fool with. Things like building decks, like the shelves I'm doing for Marty's closet—that kind of thing. I think we could make a living. Not a great one, but enough to hold us together for a while."

She didn't know. She didn't doubt he could do the work. He loved building, remodeling, adding things to the house. He'd completely built an entertainment wall in the den; cabinets he made for the kitchen cost half the original ones. But as a business . . . she didn't know.

"What say we try?"

He said "we," which was a start.

Bonnie Rose didn't really believe he'd do it, and certainly not make a living at it, but she smiled. It was one thing to know the HLBs existed. It was another to know she could handle them.

King of the Comics

MAMA MAKES ICED tea in her white-curtained closet of a kitchenette. She, who used to think small kitchens were a curse and closed her in, loves this one. She has any extra inch filled with plants. An asparagus fern brushes my head, tickles my neck. Begonias, spider plants, geraniums, others crowd out the light. Daddy used to say Mother not only had a green thumb, she had green fingers to match it. Plants are a part of my childhood; this apartment is not. Mother moved here after Daddy died, kept few things from the house, a chair, her small drop-leaf table, mirror and chest. Mostly everything is new and it is strange to me to see her here.

"I don't remember any Beasleys living on Harmon Street." She hands me a wedge of lemon, thick and large the way I have always liked it. "Lemonade," Mother used to say, "that's what you drink—not tea. Leave the tea out and be honest with it."

"The Beasleys lived in the white two-story house at the top of the hill." I drink my tart-sweet tea. An ice cube bumps my nose, chills the tip.

"You mean Clara's house," she says. "Clara sold it to—"

"No, I mean the one across from Clara's house. Beasleys. They had a maid."

"Nobody on Harmon Street ever had a maid." Mama lays her spoon on a napkin, holds up one finger. "Wait. Old Mrs. Toliver. She had a maid once. No, that was a nurse and just before she died. Poor old dear, I haven't thought about her in years."

"No, I'm sure the Beasleys had a full-time maid. She used to walk down the street early in the mornings." I remember her carrying an umbrella and shopping bag. The shopping bag bumped her legs and she used the umbrella to keep the sun off her head when she waited for the bus.

Every dog on Harmon Street yapped at her every morning. It was quiet when I walked toward the Beasleys' in the soft black tar later in the day. A broken strap on one of my sandals made me clop like a crippled horse, but the street was hot and I didn't dare take them off. I couldn't go barefooted beside the street because there were clumps of nettles, sharp, spiny things with evil-smelling yellow berries my brothers loved to shoot in their slingshots. I did better with gravel and liked the sound it made hitting something. Roger and Rich also shot chinaberries, and wild cherries. Anything to make a stink or stain, Mama said, and send one of the neighborhood kids running to her or home screaming. But that was mostly last summer. This year we were older, read a lot, played games. A single Monopoly game continued a week if the fights settled peacefully and nobody moved the board. Mostly it was comic books. "Thank the Lord for whoever invented them," Mama said. "I haven't had so much peace and quiet in the house at one time since they were all sick with the mumps."

I carefully carried a stack of comic books under my arm. "Superman" was on top, "Masked Marvel" next, "Tales of Horror." "Wild West Adventures" and "Archie," "Baby

Huey" and "Casper" on the bottom.

"Don't trade for any mush stuff," Roger said as I left. "No 'True Romance' or that junk."

"He doesn't have those," I said, and decided if he did, I'd trade for them.

"Be sure the beat-up comics are on the bottom," Rick said. "He won't notice."

"The heck he won't," Roger said, jumped and tried to touch the door frame. "He'd make you trade two of ours for one of his if you didn't watch."

I was to trade with "Bug" Beasley, since the last time Roger and Rick went they came home cheated. A rotten deal. He wouldn't take one of ours if a cover was loose, page torn or anything.

"Bug has his comics written down," Rick said. "A list on his wall. He checks off when you borrow one, knows when you bring it back. Won't trade for one he's had."

"He's crazy." Roger rolled his eyes.

"Crazy smart." Rick flexed his muscle. "His room's neat. All those planes and stuff."

The Beasleys had only lived on Harmon Street a few months. Bill was a year older than me, three years older than Roger and Rick. He played with us evenings. Games in the dark. Hide and Seek, Run Sheep Run, Snake in the Gully, Sling the Biscuit . . . games where somebody always gets hurt, Mama said. "Why do you kids think it is fun to run and scream like something crazy in the dark?"

I shifted the comic books under my arm, yanked up my elastic halter and felt my breast rub against me. Mama had been trying to put me in a bra all summer. I had held out so far and only wore one to church. Dressed up it wasn't so bad. "Boys don't wear those things," I told Mama.

"They don't have to," she said.

I made a face as she left the room.

A bra was all straps that held me down, reined me in like a horse.

On the Beasley porch, I took off my sandals, left them beside the brick steps and made dusty shadow prints as I walked the slick, gray paint to the door.

The doorbell sounded harsh over the kitchen radio tuned to "Our Gal Sunday . . . Can a young girl from a small mining town in the West find happiness as a wife of a wealthy and titled Englishman?"

"Yes," Mrs. Beasley called. Her tiny heels tapped the waxed floor toward me. Always dressed to the teeth, make-up, perfume, and dangling earrings . . . Mama said she was "artificial as a doll." Mrs. Hendon across the street said, "The rest of us could go around dressed up all day if we had someone doing our work too."

"It's Frances," I called, "Frances Bolt."

"Come in, dear." She held the door, her orange hair in curls like carrot peels covering her head.

"I came to trade comics with Bill." I shifted the books.

In the kitchen, the ironing board groaned as the maid ironed.

"Bil-lie," Mrs. Beasley called up the stairs, hand on the rail. A ring with a green stone big as a grasshopper sat on her finger.

Bill came to the top of the stairs, rubbed his head as if he'd been asleep. "Okay"—he saw the books—"if you got anything I want."

The lenses of his glasses were so thick it was hard to tell what he was thinking.

"Let me see what you got." He took my books, sat on the floor of his room, spread them around. "I've seen this one." He slid "Superman" across to me.

I studied his stamp collection framed on the walls.

He flipped "Masked Marvel" at me. "This is old. Where do you get such junk? The trash can?" He flipped another. "'Archies' . . . I don't read."

That made three strike-outs. Eight left. I wondered if he'd like any of them. Spread on his desk like a fossil were the ribs of a model airplane.

"Don't touch that," he snapped. "Glue's not dry."

I put my hands behind me.

"There's comics under the bed." Bill said. He lifted the spread, pulled several out.

I saw a "Spider Man" Roger and Rick would like, a new "Horror Tales" halfway back. I slid under to reach it. There were dust bunnies and I had to rub my nose to keep from sneezing. Mama would laugh to know that prissy Mrs. Beasley had dust balls as big as cotton bolls under her bed.

I slid out three comic books. One was "Love Secrets" but it was marked up in red ink, a mustache drawn on the guy holding the girl making kissy lips. "Five Exciting Romances in One Big Issue." If I traded for that one, Bill would have to give me two, it was so scribbled up.

Bill fell against me. I rolled over and away. "Watch . . . out . . . what are you trying to do?"

He grabbed my halter and pulled it down. His hands were hot, sticky and smelled like glue. There was brown on his nails. "Stop," I said. "Don't do that."

He kissed me hard. "Stop." I tried to twist away. His breath smelled of peanut butter and his teeth hurt. He was squeezing my breast. "That hu . . . Let me go." I squirmed under him, kicked the floor, pounded on it with my hands. The zipper on his pants bit my leg.

He grabbed my wrist and as he loosened the grip on my mouth, I bit his finger so hard I felt the bone crunch between my teeth.

"You bitch," he screamed, "you little bitch."

I scrambled up, pulled my clothes on, and flung comic books right and left, pages ripping.

Bill sat beside the bed, looked at his finger. "Look what you did. You made it bleed."

I dived out the door, half fell down the stairs, almost bumped into the maid on the landing.

"What's the trouble?" she puffed. "What's going on up

there? You kids—"

I swung past her and out. Halfway home I noticed my feet burning and remembered my sandals. I wouldn't have gone back for them if they'd been gold.

In the kitchen, I flung down the comic books, ran to my room.

Roger and Rick spilled sugar, stirred Kool-Aid. "Hey, these look like ours—You didn't—"

I locked my door, hit my bed, and cried hard into the pillow. I didn't care if it soaked through and I had to sleep on it wet. Bug Beasley was the worst boy in the world. I hated him. I didn't want breasts if boys pulled and hurt them. Roger and Rick pounded my door, yelled, "Open up." They finally went away.

Mother knocked then. "Are you sick? What's wrong?"

I didn't answer.

She got a skeleton key and came in. What good was a lock if anybody could get a key and come in any time they wanted? I cried harder.

"Does your stomach hurt?" Mama whispered.

"It's not that," I said.

My periods had started three months before and I was afraid. At first I thought I was dying. That I would bleed to death. "Hush," Mama said, "it's part of growing up." She showed me how to wear a belt like another harness and pad of a saddle between my legs. It was awful. I couldn't walk. Felt bowlegged. "All part of being a girl," Mama said. "You get used to it."

"I don't want it," I whined. "I don't want to be a girl."

"I'm afraid you don't have any choice." She had a sad, odd smile.

I lay on my side, studied my postcard collection on the wall. The one of the Empire State Building, as high as I could go, then France, as far as I could go . . . and away from Bill Beasley.

Mama ran water in the bathroom, came back with a cool

cloth. She folded it across my forehead. "What happened?"

I told her Bill Beasley tried to pull my clothes off.

"You didn't let him," she said with a gasp.

"No," I said, "I pushed him away."

"Where was this? Where did it happen?"

"In his room."

"What were you doing in his room?"

"Trading comic books."

"You shouldn't have gone to his room," she said.

"That's where the comic books were."

"You should have made him bring them downstairs then." She acted mad at me.

"It's not my—"

"Where was his mother?"

"Downstairs," I said, "in the living room."

"The whole time?" Mama said.

"Yes—and the maid was—"

"If you had been wearing a bra," Mama said, "this would not have happened."

"Get out," I told Mama. "Go away and leave me alone."

I cried some more and slept. Daddy brought me supper on a tray. Macaroni-n-Cheese and a Jello salad. Mama had made gingerbread with lemon icing for dessert. She knew I liked it. I didn't touch it.

Daddy talked while I ate, promised me we'd go riding this weekend, that he thought I was big enough to handle one of the other horses and old Ted was too slow. He never mentioned it, but I knew he knew. Mama told him everything. Always.

I heard her later on the phone. "No, I don't think Frances has an active imagination. I'm sure she wouldn't make up a story like this. She has no reason . . ."

"Frances is not that kind . . . Well, what kind of boy are you raising to do a thing like this? Oh, I'm sure your precious Bill always tells you the truth . . . that he would never touch . . ."

Ask the maid, I wanted to say through the door, she'll tell you. She saw my clothes . . .

"If that's the way you want it," Mama snapped. I heard her slam the receiver in its cradle with a jolt. "Forget it, forget the whole thing."

"Like mother, like son," she said to Daddy later. "I might have known."

"You are not to go near that house," Mama told me the next day. "And if you see Bill Beasley, you come home fast."

Roger and Rick giggled. They had no idea what happened, I am sure. Probably thought it was because of the comic books.

"And another thing," Mama said after the boys went out. "You are not to leave this house again without a bra."

"Never," I said.

"Never."

I put on the bra and an old blouse with roll-up sleeves. Stayed in my room a lot, reading. At night Roger and Rick, the other kids would yell for me to come play Hide and Seek.

"Leave her alone," Mama said. "She's getting too big to be out running around in the dark. Somebody is going to get hurt yet."

I knew what she thought. That if Bill Beasley was out there he'd grab me again. I hated him, hated, hated.

From my room, I could see his room, a light on at night. Sometimes he undressed and didn't pull the shade.

When I saw the moving van backed up to the Beasleys' a week or so later, Mama said, "Good riddance," and I echoed her in my head.

I never knew what happened to the maid. Surely she had no trouble finding another job. Good maids were hard to find then as now. No one else in the neighborhood hired her or ever had a maid. Even in time of sickness, they helped each other.

"Everyone but Mrs. Hendon has moved from the old

neighborhood," Mama says now as she sits across from me in this greenhouse of a kitchen. "The day they bulldozed down our house, Lou Hendon called me to come watch. I asked her what for? It's not part of me anymore. What do I care if they tear it down, build apartments?"

I care, I started to say. A part of me is being flattened out, erased, rumbled over, covered. My childhood and more. Some parts I want to erase, yet they sprout like rubble.

"Have you driven down Harmon Street since you've been home?" Mama asks.

"Yesterday, as I was going to the shopping center." Only the willow tree stood where our house had been. The rest of the lot was flat, waiting. The Beasley house was the same, shiny wedding-cake white. Porch floor polished now as then and there were fluffy ferns in white wicker stands.

"The maid's name was Radie," Mama says. The word pops from her mouth like a fruit pit. "That was her name."

I know then that Mama remembers. Remembers the Beasleys, Bill, the whole business.

She doesn't look at me, instead reaches up and crumbles off a brown leaf from one of the begonias. She pokes the soil to see if it needs watering. "When you go, take some of these plants with you. I'm crowded out of this apartment—there's not room for them all."

I feel that way now about bad memories. I don't have room for them all. They crowd my life and cause blight. And as I leave, two begonias and a rose geranium in my arms, I lean back to kiss Mother's cheek, something I haven't done in a long time. It's all right, I want to say. I love you. She waves as I start down the stairs. She knows.

The Silver Crescent

IF MY GRANDMOTHER were alive today and I gave her a pair of pantyhose, she'd unwrap them, examine the package front and back, thank me graciously, and hand them back. And if I protested, she'd say, "Honey, I never wear them."

"But Grandma," I'd say.

"I wouldn't know how to put the things on in the first place," she'd say, "and you know I don't like any stockings but silk."

And I'd remember. Yes, I ought to know. To know very well. That was all I heard the summer I was thirteen. She and Aunt Rennie.

Every fifteen minutes they came in: "Are you asleep yet?" And when I said "No," they'd say, "Well, you better be, because it's going to be a long night."

I felt like it had been a long night already. I hummed songs, told myself stories, leaned out the window, listened to dogs bark and cats howl. Just after I closed my eyes, Aunt Rennie woke me saying, "Hurry, hurry, trains don't wait."

If the Silver Crescent had been a horse it would have snorted, stamped its legs, and whisked its tail to be off. Instead the doors stood open and my grandmother clutched her black leather-strapped suitcase like a life preserver.

"Give it to the porter," Aunt Rennie said gently.

"No." Grandma tightened her grip and her mouth.

The porter in his navy blue uniform and red cap bowed at the waist, touched his cap. "Ma'am."

"No." Grandmother stepped back.

"But why, Mama?" Rennie moved closer. "It's his job. You don't want that thing in your way the whole trip."

"He can't have it." Grandmother rearranged her sweater across her shoulders, tightened her grip on the suitcase handle. "I might not get it back." She eyed the waiting porter, who crossed his ankles, tugged the tip of his small, curled black mustache.

"Of course you will." Rennie was exasperated now. "I've never heard of such a thing, have you, Patsy?"

I shrugged. It was my first train trip too. Aunt Rennie had gone to New York twice a year since she started working for Foto's Department Store in Fairmont. Buying Trips, she called them in capital letters. She ran the millinery department at Foto's and all year long she'd hold up some hat like a freshly decorated cake on a plate and tell Mrs. Foto and her friends she thought of them the minute she laid eyes on this hat in New York City. That it was perfect for them and she couldn't imagine anyone else in town wearing it. Then she'd whisper that of course it was an original, a one-of-a-kind, and whoever bought it would never have to worry about meeting herself coming *or* going in Fairmont, or anywhere else for that matter.

The ladies would buy the hats, leave in a swirl of gold-striped and corded boxes. Mr. Foto would take out his half-cigar and with the handkerchief from his pocket would wipe his oily, brown, and balding head. Aunt Rennie was tall, gray, and fifty, but she knew women and hats and everyone in Fairmont, so Dick Foto staked her to the New York trips.

I imagined Aunt Rennie in New York. She'd be like she was anywhere, hatted, of course, usually a large one with flowers or a trailing feather and always her pink umbrella folded tight as a fresh petunia and ruffling at the handle. With the sharp tip she got attention, sometimes by poking people in the chest. I'd seen her poke Louis Mehew. "Young man," she said, "if that's gum you're chewing, I'd advise you to stop the nasty habit right now if you know what's good for you." And Louis gulped down his gum.

Now Aunt Rennie aimed that same arrow of an umbrella off the side of Grandma, whispered loudly, "For Lord's sake, Mama, you're holding up the whole train, making a spectacle . . . let the man have your suitcase."

Grandma loosened her grip, finger by finger. The porter eased it from her and, almost tripping, ran to the baggage car.

"That's the last I'll ever see of my suitcase," Grandma said in a little-girl voice. "I know bad blood when I see it."

"Ohhhhh . . ." Rennie blew out her breath like steam. "He's in a hurry because you held up the train. Of all the ign—He's putting it on the baggage car beside my suitcase, with Patsy's. With everybody else's who's already on this train. And if we don't get on soon . . ." She pushed Grandma up the narrow metal stairs. "We've been laughed at enough. See if you can find a seat without another commotion."

I looked around. There was no one on the train platform. At 2:00 a.m. the whole town was as deserted as any small town in the South. Nobody had laughed at us. I giggled. Aunt Rennie reached a hand back, grabbed me, and yanked just at the train shuffled, blew a stinging skirt of sand, and started off.

We stumbled into the car as the train lurched, released brakes in a scratch of metal. Grandma toppled into the first seat atop a sleeping fat man who snorted, "What? What is this?"

"Not there." Rennie pulled. "You don't want a seat back

here. Let's get one where you and Patsy can be together. Don't sit with strangers."

We wove toward the front, past people with pillows, seats tilted, heads back and mouths open like fish. Some slept curled in their seat, others sprawled, dangled arms in the aisles.

The dark was heavy as a cape and sparks shot from under the wheels like firecrackers.

I sat bolt upright beside Grandma stiff in her best navy blue crepe with the lace collar. Not even red silk roses on her hat wiggled. She could have been one of Foto's Department Store mannequins, still as she sat.

The train moaned through an occasional town, rocked easy as any toy horse. New York was a world away.

Across the aisle, Aunt Rennie promptly went to sleep. She snored like a grinding motor. I hoped nobody knew she was with us.

Grandma and I made a mirror picture in the train window. I saw the part in my hair, touched my birthday string of pearls from Belk's, and posed with my neck arched, chest out in my white dotted Swiss dress and ballerina skirt ruffling around me. I wore white socks and black patent-leather shoes, my first with heels. On my ankle, a bracelet of two hearts initialed PM and BH, Buddy Harkey. He'd given it to me for my birthday. Mama said not to wear the bracelet next to my skin or it would leave a green ring.

Riding the train at night was like going into a tunnel only you never came out. I kept looking, waiting for the light at the end, but it never came. I pretended it was at the movies and I waited for the picture to start, but there was nothing but people breathing and the everlasting black flannel.

My seat prickled under me and the linen napkin behind my head was stiff as paper. The whole train was a rolling box of snores. Finally Grandma said, "I coulda kept it at my feet."

"What?" I looked at her.

"My suitcase," she said. "No reason to let him have it."

Lights outside the window winked at me and once I saw the silhouette of a horse on a hill. I drifted to sleep and woke to find Grandma hadn't moved a breath. She still stared at the gray wall in front of the car, held her purse hard in her lap, the clasp with both hands.

The conductor came through, punched our tickets, tipped his cap to Grandma. "Have a good trip, ma'am."

She smiled a little, nodded her roses.

Outside, the sky greened in streaks, became orange and pink silk. A few people in the car lifted green shades at their windows, yawned, stretched. One man opened his briefcase, took out a razor, and shaved. I felt embarrassed, as though I had seen someone in a private act. Several people took trips to the bathroom, came back tugging ties, patting down freshly combed hair, headed for the dining car. I'd wanted to eat in the dining car but Aunt Rennie said, "Who can afford it? Not me. We got more sense than pay six prices for things just because it's a train we're on."

I would have settled for a Coke, but Rennie and Grandma had packed a lunch the night before in a hatbox with cellophane see-through on top.

Aunt Rennie woke, rustled in her box, passed across chicken, ham biscuits, deviled eggs, chocolate cake.

Grandma held the chicken toward me. I shook my head.

"You got to eat." She took a dark bite off a drumstick, nicked the bone. "You don't know when you'll get another chance."

Grandma chewed loud. The whole train echoed and the sulphur smell of eggs made me turn away. I hoped nobody knew where the smell came from.

Aunt Rennie kept passing across food. I kept refusing. Grandma ate.

Finally I took a plum, a handful of green grapes, cool and wet in my hand. "You'll get that juice on your dress," Grandma warned, "and it won't come out."

I cupped my hand under the plum, bit deep and sucked the red sour juice that tasted good down to my toes.

A group of people got off the train at a small yellow station in Virginia. I tried to read the name of the town but couldn't. They reached overhead for briefcases, boxes, paper bags with handles as they left.

"I coulda kept mine," Grandma said. "They're back there going through it."

"Why would anyone go through your suitcase?" I asked.

"Money." Grandma rounded the word. "What else?" She patted her breast and paper rattled. "I fooled them. I got mine pinned to me."

I saw two shining stitches of safety pins small in her dress. In my suitcase, I'd packed six Bit-O-Honey bars and some Juicy Fruit gum. If they were missing, I'd know Grandma was right.

Aunt Rennie passed us a damp paper towel to wipe our hands and pass back. She folded everything back in the cake box, tied it with gold cord, and got into a long conversation with her seatmate, a widow from Pleasant Grove. I heard Aunt Rennie tell about Foto's and what a perfectly lovely little town Fairmont was and how she'd have to come visit when the dogwoods bloomed. That she'd only be in New York three days, but Grandma and I would be with her sister, my Aunt Lucille, and Uncle Taylor in Trenton for two weeks. They lived in New Jersey. They way she said New Jersey I knew it wasn't as good or as important as New York, but Aunt Lucille had written if I'd come with Grandma they'd take me sightseeing. Since Uncle Taylor was a Ford dealer, I figured we'd go a lot and Trenton was farther from North Carolina than I'd ever been.

We changed trains in Washington and that worried Aunt Rennie. The Crescent didn't go any further north, she said.

I didn't see what Rennie was so worried about since the conductor took us right to the other train, helped Grandma get settled. She hissed, "Is my suitcase still on that train?"

"No, no," Rennie said. "They switch everything. Now hush."

She told me to wait until we got out of town to use the bathroom and cross my legs and hold it if I had to. I edged past her and walked the aisle like a plank until I reached the bathroom with its pink sink the size of Ruthie's playhouse one. Grandma would say this room wasn't big enough to cuss a cat in. I giggled. When I flushed I saw the track riding gray and steel under me and grass, shiny bits of metal.

Aunt Rennie helped Grandma, her hand under her elbow guiding and Grandma saying, "I'm fine," and pulling away.

They came back with their hats on straight, hair freshly combed, and gloves smooth.

As the train eased toward the station and between other trains, I held my breath it seemed so close. Like we were sliding into a slot. Aunt Rennie was ready. "I'll help you out," she told Grandma.

"My suitcase . . ." Grandma said.

"It's with the others, for goodness sakes." Rennie waved to Lucille.

Aunt Lucille hugged us, got lipstick on my collar. She smelled of narcissus and cherry blossoms. "Be good," she called to Rennie, and Rennie yelled back, "And if I can't be good, I'll be careful." They both laughed loud. I wanted to stand behind a post but there wasn't one.

"I want mine." Grandma walked toward the suitcases on the platform.

In the rack of suitcases, I saw my plaid zippered one and pulled it out.

"It isn't here." Grandma said and bent, read tags. "I know it isn't."

Lucille picked up a black one. "This looks like yours."

"Well, it's not." Grandma reached for the tag, turned it over. "See, I know my own suitcase."

Lucille put it down, called a porter, had him check the luggage.

Grandma fidgeted, fussed. "I knew all the time something was going to happen. Never should have let it from my sight."

Lucille checked inside the station, came back frowning. "They said some luggage was left on the other train by mistake and your suitcase must have been one of those."

"Oh," Grandma moaned. "Now he's got it and he'll just keep it. Everything in the world I had to wear."

"It's supposed to be on the next train," Lucille said.

"Lord knows when that will be." Grandma rolled her eyes toward the ceiling.

"Three o'clock," Lucille said. "We might as well have some lunch, kill some time until then."

Grandma wouldn't eat the club sandwich Lucille ordered for her. She complained the mayonnaise was old. I had a toasted cheese and licked the melted threads between bites. Lucille only had black coffee and worried about her office. "I told them I might be a little late getting back"—she rubbed out her cigarette—"but not the whole blessed afternoon."

"I knew all along this would happen," Grandma said to anyone in the room.

We waited on a bench in the station until four o'clock and every parcel of luggage had been unloaded and checked. I knew all the cracks in the wall, ceiling. There was a map of Italy in the corner, overhead the Mississippi River.

When we left with only my suitcase, Grandma sank into Lucille's car, fanned herself with her hand. "Here I am in this Godforsaken place without a stitch to my name but what I got on."

"They said they'd find it and have it delivered tomorrow." Lucille started the hot car, backed from the parking place.

Grandma and I had twin beds in the pink wallpapered guest room. Grandma paced while I unpacked, gave her the top drawers in the bureau. "I don't know what for," she mumbled.

After dinner she said she guessed she'd have to just sleep in her dress.

Lucille, loading the dishwasher, said, "Mama, I'll get you some of my gowns, a robe, slippers and things. Just give me time."

"I'll rinse out my step-ins," she said, "and hang them in the upstairs bath. They ought to dry overnight—as hot as it is up there."

"If worse comes to worse"—Lucille scraped a plate—"you can always buy a few things. It won't hurt you to have a new dress or two."

"I *had* a new dress," Grandma said from the stairs. "Rennie got it for me at Foto's. Green with blue and white stripes. Not worn yet. Price tag still on it. No telling who's wearing it now."

"It's for sure that porter isn't," I said.

She gave me a dark look. "Probably got a wife that is. I don't trust anybody whose eyes are too far apart. One look and I knew."

The next day, Lucille took us shopping in a big, bright, flower garden–smelling department store. I rode the escalator about a dozen times. Grandma wouldn't get on and Lucille went in the elevator with her. She didn't want to buy anything, and none of the things she looked at were as well-made or as pretty as what she had in her suitcase. She did buy one dress and some underwear, a nightgown. "A change," she said, rolling down the top of the silver-colored bag.

"Something you could use, anyway," Lucille said. "Don't begrudge it."

Grandma fussed. "No use spending money on things I already had. If I'd just let my common sense rule . . ."

Uncle Taylor took us to Radio City Music Hall. "I've never seen a Rockette I didn't like." He winked at Aunt Lucille.

At the top of the Empire State Building, Grandma wouldn't get near enough to the rail to look over and held the tail of my dress, yelled the whole time for me to stay back. "She couldn't fall if she tried," Uncle Taylor laughed. "The rail's eight feet high and glass-enclosed."

I bought postcards, wrote all my friends and Buddy Harkey every day the first week. Aunt Lucille introduced me to Lisa Ponte, who lived three houses down and was fourteen. Lisa introduced me to the rest of the kids in the neighborhood, including Ronnie Martinez, who had the blackest hair and eyes I had ever seen. When he smiled, I almost lost my balance. "I don't know much about those kids," Lucille said. "They seem awfully fresh to me."

They loved my southern accent and begged me to talk and talk. They thought "you all" was supposed to be in every sentence and I had to start saying it all the time. When we went out for pizza, they made me order and the girl couldn't understand a word I said, we laughed so much.

In Atlantic City, I rode the ferris wheel out the roof and looked hard and deep toward North Carolina, couldn't see a speck. Lisa helped me buy short shorts and an elastic halter like hers. Grandma said, "If your daddy knew you were running around parading everything you got, he'd jerk you home fast."

I wasn't planning to ever go home.

Grandma spent her time washing out underwear and moaning. She wrote all her friends back home about thieving Yankees who wanted to rob an old woman of every stitch she owned. Next she worried about me going wild. She said New Jersey people looked strange, talked funny, too fast. She couldn't understand but every other word they said and I was getting to sound just like them. She said I ought to hear myself talk.

I stuck out my tongue when she turned her back.

Aunt Lucille had called the railroad every day since we'd been there and they had done everything they could to trace Grandma's suitcase.

"Trace," Grandma shouted. *"Find* is more the word."

Ten days after the suitcase was lost the railroad called to

say it had been found—in Florida.

"It couldn't have gone any farther," Grandma sneered, "or it would've been in the ocean."

"I told you the whole time," Lucille said, "things don't just disappear and people don't go around stealing suitcases."

"Humph," Grandma said, adjusting her glasses on her nose. "You just wait and see. It could be stark empty. He could have taken everything he wanted and sent back the rest."

The suitcase was delivered by special messenger and the first thing Grandma did was check the lock. "It's been opened," she said triumphantly. She examined her dresses, still folded flat and careful, counted her "step-ins," slips, nightgowns, her "good" robe and sweater. Then she patted the elastic pouch on the suitcase divider. "Not one," she said, "not the first one."

"What?" Lucille and I peered around her and into the suitcase.

"Stockings," she said. "I had a dozen new pair—never been out of their wrappers and there's not a one left—not a sign of them." Her face was long, mournful, ready to melt.

"What in the world is a few pair of stockings after all this time?" Lucille snapped. "You got your suitcase back, the rest of your things in perfect condition. I don't want to hear any more about *any* of it."

Grandma sighed, set her suitcase on the luggage rack that had been waiting empty almost two weeks. She put things in it to take home. "No use to unpack now, when I'd just have to pack again."

When she wasn't worrying about what to do with her suitcase on the trip home, Grandma perked up a little, tried to have a good time, let Uncle Taylor take us out to eat, said she'd had a fine visit in spite of everything.

Lucille winced at that, but didn't say anything.

Uncle Taylor ordered another glass of beer for everybody and a Coke refill for me.

"Beer?" Grandma said. "Was that what I had?" Her mouth hung open like a pocket. "I thought somebody up here sure didn't know how to make iced tea so it didn't cloud and bitter."

We all laughed and Grandma laughed so hard she hiccuped.

On the way to the train station, Grandma pulled her handkerchief between her fingers. I saw it becoming a string by the time we got there. "I'm going to keep it with me," she said, "if I have to sit on it the whole trip."

"Okay, okay," Lucille said. She rolled down her window and took a ticket from the parking attendant.

"And if I see that porter again, I'm going to go right up and demand to know what he meant by stealing my stockings?"

"For goodness sakes, Mama," Lucille said, "you don't know for sure. Anything could have happened."

"I bet he sold them."

"Porters are well paid." Lucille held the door, carried the suitcase. "They don't need your stockings. Black markets went out with the war."

We sat with the suitcases while Grandma went to the ladies' room. She told me I'd be sorry if I didn't go now and I said, "But I don't have to."

"I don't have to either," she said, "but I'm going anyway."

"I know it seems like she's made a big fuss over this," Lucille said. "And I hope it hasn't spoiled your trip."

I said it hadn't and touched my gold locket with the picture of Ronnie Martinez inside, felt the card with his address in my pocket.

"Don't feel too hard toward her." Lucille reached over and touched my arm. "You've never had to do without like she has, Patsy. During the war you couldn't get so many things and she hasn't ever forgotten, I guess. Stockings were prized so highly you wouldn't believe it. They could have been gold instead of silk and she still refuses to wear any but silk stockings. Everyone has something that having a lot of, makes them feel wealthy, secure, whatever—be it stockings—or gold."

Grandma held tight her suitcase, slid it on the train herself, into our seats, and popped her feet on it fast.

Aunt Lucille hugged and kissed us. "Don't wait so long to come back," she said.

"I'll see you next summer." I winked.

Grandma said, "Now you take care and write more than you been."

Lucille waved from the platform.

The porter came by, motioned to Grandma. "You'll have more room if we put that overhead."

"I'll thank you not to touch my things," she snapped.

"Yes ma'am." He touched his cap. "Yes, *ma'am.*"

"I'm going to tell Daddy you sassed somebody," I sang.

"Watch out, young lady." Grandma settled her purse in her lap flat as a book. "I know more than a *few* things that could get you sent to your room for a month."

I settled back in my seat, watched the backs of buildings, warehouses, and auto junkyards roll past.

"I hope I see whoever hires and fires people on this railroad," Grandma mumbled, looking around. "I'll tell him he can't do much of a business with thieves for help."

"Grandma"—I patted her hand—"that's all behind us now. Let's don't talk about it again."

I felt very grown up, sixteen at least. Or twenty. Traveled and celebrated . . . and kind.

The train slid through cities and the green fields of Virginia, tobacco fields and the open blue skies of North Carolina. I breathed deep, cleaned my lungs, and shouted inside my head, "I'm home, I'm home."

When we neared the station, I saw in a dizzy sea of faces someone that looked like Mama and Daddy beside her and my little brother, Robbie.

Grandma got off first, pushed her suitcase at them and told Daddy to take it and not let go for a minute. He looked puzzled.

Everybody hugged us and began a second round. Robbie smelled like damp hair, soap, and popcorn. "Did you bring me a baseball pennant from Yankee Stadium?" he asked.

"Wait and see," I said. The only thing I had brought him was a T-shirt that said Atlantic City and a Confederate Flag beach towel.

I started talking about the Rockettes and Atlantic City and Daddy almost hit the car in front of us. "Hold on." He turned around. "Do you hear her? She's been gone two weeks and come back talking just like a Yankee. I got a good notion to send her back where they talk such stuff."

"You'll do no such thing." Mama reached an arm back and pushed my bangs off my forehead. "That's an awful thing to say about your own flesh and blood."

"My flesh and blood don't talk Yankee." Daddy slammed on brakes for a stop sign.

I didn't say anything else, except in whispers to Robbie. At supper I asked Mama to pass the butter for my corn on the cob and Daddy gave me a hard look with the corner of his eye. Robbie giggled.

When I unpacked I couldn't find the beach towel I bought for Robbie.

I leaned in the door of Grandma's room. "Did I put Robbie's towel in your suitcase?"

She stood at her round old oak dresser with the black teardrop pulls. She turned with a white look and something in her hand.

"It was like a flag," I said.

She tried to push the colored packages in her hand back into the small drawer that hung half-open.

"Those look like—" I started.

"Well, they're not," Grandma said. "I had them in that back pocket in my suitcase. They were the last thing I put in and—never mind."

I didn't know what to say.

"Nobody's perfect," Grandma said. She straightened the

crocheted scarf on her dresser, rearranged her jars and bottles, the velvet pincushion. "Nobody in this world ever got through life without making a mistake."

I kissed her powdered and violet-smelling neck and tiptoed out.

She died the year I was eighteen and I wonder often what she would have said about my husband, Carlos. Whatever, she would adore our little Rosita Ann.

He Holds a Black Umbrella

At my door

TWO SCRUBBED ALL-AMERICAN boys, white shirts, ties, wire-rimmed glasses, crew-cut hair the color of wheatfield stubble. They bow, smile as if waiting for a camera to click. Elder Jones and Elder Richardson at your service, ma'am. Elder? I think Younger. Tweedledum and Tweedledee. Dum has a black tooth and smiles crookedly to try to cover. I wonder how they let him in the Order of the Church of Yesterday's Saints with so obvious a flaw? Elder Jones asks if they can come in, give me God's Message For Today. They have a card with a picture of Jesus ascending. White clouds, gold halo. Blue Sky. A memento of the visit. A weather chart. The card sky is blue today. When it turns pink there is a chance of rain. The charts really work and are nice to hang on your wall, Elder Jones says. Elder Richardson admires his fine shined shoes, pats four fingers on his Bible, impatient to be on with The Word. May they come in for a moment? I am busy, it has been a rough morning. The dishwasher stuck, but its pump did not. Flooded the floor. My tile may buckle. Too bad, they say, to be too busy to take time to hear the Scriptures. My child has eased out the door and reaches for the weather chart/Jesus card. They hold it away from his sticky hand. The card can only be left after a visit. They walk across my yard, leave a wake of bent grass, a brushed path. Next door I hear the other Elder take his turn. Good day, ma'am. Good luck. Next door lives the World's Champion Bitch. I take my child into his room, give him crayons, an index card, tell him to make a weather chart.

It is raining

my husband is reading *Walden,* Thoreau's Words for Today. He reads aloud. I am reading Can This Marriage Be Saved. Sometimes in bed he reads Walden aloud. This is his third reading. Thoreau is not good in bed. The children are asleep. The stereo plays An Evening with Bach Harpsichord and Cello. The record finishes flips and Johnny Cash moans he is so lonesome he could die. My husband does not look up from *Walden,* but his eyebrow does. Variety, I say, is the herb and sinew of life. I decide to make coffee, perked coffee; let it smell good long. Tease my senses. Like sex, half the enjoyment is in the anticipation. The doorbell rings and out my rainy porthole I see night, a wash of street lights and empty streets. I open the door to a child. A girl of perhaps nine or ten. Her dark hair is matted, limp across the soiled imitation-fur collar of a too-short coat. She holds a used paper bag both hands tight around its neck as though it is alive and might try to escape. I think of drawings of street urchins, round-eyed children, stray kittens, and want to let her in. She reaches inside her bag, hands me a torn slip of paper. My Father, she says, wants you to read this. Against the rain and Johnny Cash, her voice is a whisper. Has there been an accident? Her father injured and she has come to my house for help? I unfold the slip of lined paper and read the dark pencil scrawl, "For God so loved the world, He gave His only begotten Son." I read it twice, ask where her father is. Out there. She points down the street. I step onto the porch. Cold dampness makes me shiver, wrap myself with my arms. I see nothing. Can you come in? He won't let me, she says. My Father wouldn't like it. What would he say? He tells people about Jesus' Love and how he came to save the world. My Father is a Preacher. I have to go now. She snatches the paper back, runs down the street. Under a misting globe, I see a man. He holds a black umbrella.

In the Safeway supermarket

a woman in a blue smock imprinted *We Care* stocks the dairy case. I reach for cottage cheese. She hands me a carton. I thank her. We discuss the price of meat, the state of the world. She says she has quit going to church. Last week was her last time. Preachers, she says, do not bless our boys in service anymore. They do not pray for them in their Sunday prayers. Just because there is not a war on does not mean our boys do not need praying for. I take a box of margarine and say the special on real butter is real good. At the register line, I unload the grocery cart; lettuce, carrots, a can of peas. Onions, potatoes, a potted plant, a package of pantyhose, Moonlight Petite One Size Fits All. My child reaches from his cart seat and takes a small red book from a bird feeder display. The New Gospel in Miniature. Free. Take One. He chews. Red drips down his chin, onto his shirt, stains his hands. I put the book back and buy him candy. A small line under the Free says $1 donations will be accepted for the Continuing Ministry and appreciated. I wonder if the red will wash out, if the dye is safe, if my son will be sick? Stopped for a traffic light, the yellow pickup truck in front has an empty gun rack across its rear window, is driven by a vanilla-haired lady. Her left bumper sticker says God Is Not Dead I Talked to Him This Morning. Her right bumper sticker says Prayer Is the Answer. My son hits the horn. In her mirror, the driver gives me a peace sign, a faceful of black exhaust. Even God cannot breathe. At home I open the cottage cheese and see green fuzz mold. The freshness date guarantees next week. I feed it to the dog, tell him penicillin is made from mold and he will never have an infection, live forever.

Having lunch with a friend

she blesses our tuna fish sandwiches. I haven't read the papers today and wonder if tuna is the latest ban. God is great. She folds her hands like the picture in a child's prayer book. God is good. There is a dog hair, stiff as a bristle, in my sandwich. Under the table Mollie the Collie bumps my feet, clicks her teeth as she bites fleas. God we thank him for this food. She shows me a cookbook put out by the Ladies Church Circle. $4.50. Did it themselves, even turned the mimeo by hand. There are recipes for Black Pepper Cake, Radish Pie, Celery Pudding. I dread dessert. By his hands.

After the fifth phone call

I accept the invitation. Dinner for two. Free. No charge to you as Guests of the Great American Land Developers Association. We wear our sales resistance armor. The male Cheerleader at my elbow tries. He has scored with the other couple at our table. Newlyweds. Six months, already the owners of a Piece of Paradise. She wears a yellow floral corsage. Mr. Cheerleader makes a great show of pinning it to her chest. I feel left out of the May Court, flowerless. The newlyweds rent an apartment, lease furniture, but have been thinking toward retirement, put their down payment on Florida Forests Forever. During dinner they talk golf. Mr. Cheerleader asks if we play. No, my husband says. Sail? No again. Swim? Boat? Fish? Three more nos. Then he asks exactly what my husband does do. He reads, I say. Reads! Cheerleader is astonished. Reads, he repeats. Reads. He meets all kinds of nuts in this business but this is a new one. During dinner the new bride snaps at her husband because he got catsup on his tie. He snips back. I wonder who gets payments on Paradise in a divorce settlement? The attraction of the evening is unveiled. The Head Cheerleader gyrates with his roving microphone. Hip hip hooray. They show slides of Paradise. Grass, birds, trees and breeze. The GALDA made the waters and firmaments and found they were good and have not rested. Let's hear it for payments of $83.09 a week for the rest of your life. The giant green kidney of a map is cheered. We can buy a square as big as a Chiclet beside the golf course, adjoining the country club, on the lake, across the canal. We have a Chapel, says Cheerleader, for all faiths. A different door for each. Jewish, Catholic, Protestant. Which are you? Waldenites, I say, and Cheerleader says we have that too. There are many unmarked doors in Paradise. Invest, he urges, double, triple, googolplex your money. Send your son to college. Why, my husband asks. He can already read. We leave without a tip and the waitress blocks Cheerleader's stride after us. On the way home, a billboard proclaims in sparkle letters the Second Coming of Christ. Everyone is invited, but only ticketholders will be admitted. Underneath is a picture of Billy Graham, and the dates May 20–25.

Cows, Coathangers, and the K-Mart Kid

The Voice

EACH NEIGHBORHOOD MUST have a single voice. One nobody would claim. A sound you'd hear if you put your ear to the ground in the middle of the night. A chatty, busybody, gossipy, snippy sort of barnyard voice that is heard when people live too close and pick, pick, pick into each other's lives.

The Green Pastures That Became Ashwood Heights

Subdivisions are all alike. Call them Merry Hope Runs, or Cricket Hops, or Hobble Horse Hills, they're pretty standard. Planned and priced to the square inch, brick, boards, trees, and turf. Models of American Pie. The people too are pretty much the same. Salt, pure salt of the earth. But this story is about grass, the folding green, mowing green, fertilizing and airing green of suburban kind. And what salt does to grass. And one house in a neighborhood. You've seen those houses. Black sheep in a family, ill-fated from the first, the unusual, the pieces that don't fit in the Norman Rockwell picture puzzle.

In Ashwood Heights the kids call it "the bad house." It was the last to be sold and stood empty almost a year after the others became curtained and mailboxed and fenced, with petunias in their identical planters. The bad house's yard went to seed. Its shrubs died. Its one stick tree got broken off even with the ground. It was a disgrace. Bettye Cobb, who lived on one side, and Sally Zimmer, who lived on the other, worried that this house contaminated the whole neighborhood. They looked and talked about it as if bricks and boards could spread some contagious disease to their own dear yards and loved ones. Bettye and Sally spent mornings and afternoons while their babies napped drinking coffee in each other's kitchens. If their husbands were out of town, they often slipped over with some sewing or embroidery, going back every fifteen minutes to check on Stevie or Susie, deep asleep in their cribs. The bad house between them was an eyesore, a pox. Their dozen trips daily across its yard packed it hard, wore a path in the pale, thin grass. Both said the house was an absolute disgrace and the city should do something. The developer should do something. *Somebody* had to do something.

The Farmer's Wife

When someone learned that the bad house had been sold, excitement went around the neighborhood like a twenty-four-hour virus. In a day or two a truck backed up, started to unload. A small car from some unknown country, the color of a stray cat, parked in front. It had a cracked windshield on the passenger side and the rear window was broken, replaced by a cardboard that read "Kotex" in four places. Sally was over with her Good Neighbor pot of coffee and some fresh, home-baked sweet rolls, "last year's winner in the Bake-Off" recipe. Before the car doors shut the family pooch, a cross between collie and German shepherd, marked the front door.

"Those people," she said to Bettye, "those people ... I don't know how to say it ... but they're hicks. Pure hicks. God knows where they came from and what they're doing here—in *our* neighborhood. I wouldn't think they've got enough sense, much less money, to sign a mortgage agreement."

Bettye sniffed with one nostril. "I think we may have been better with the house empty." She had never thought she'd say those words.

Moving boxes stayed in the yard two months. Kids flattened them to slide the slope in the front yard. No sooner than a garbage man would cart one off, aided by Sally or Bettye who took turns stealing out in the dark of midnight to stack them on the curb and pray from their windows for early pick-up, than the kids pulled out more. They spent hours sliding and squealing down the brown slopes. If they had toys, no one ever saw them. They played with things like brooms, mops, pans, spoons, curtains, sheets, and old furniture. Sofas and chairs sat in the yard like old people with sagging stomachs. Cotton and packing hung out like intestines. In the yard the furniture was rained upon, left to rot. Bettye and Sally almost gagged every time they looked at it. "Isn't there a law against stuff like that? "Surely there is." "There must be."

Jack and Jill, the two oldest Farmer children—yes, their name was Farmer—looked like twins. Lottie Farmer told Sally they were ten months and two weeks apart. "Don't let anyone tell you that you can't get pregnant when you're nursing. Because I'm the living proof."

"Oh, I wouldn't," said Sally. "I wouldn't for anything."

She put her hands in the air. Her eyes were dark as nipples.

The Farmer baby, called Boo, was a year younger than Jack. If she had another name, no one ever heard it. They were always called Jack and Jill and Boo like a nursery rhyme that was wrong.

All three children, like Lottie, were thin as rags. They had frog eyes the color of pond water and Saran Wrap–like hair. Their noses continually ran and they coughed constantly, not hack-hack coughs, but deep, retching, dark-colored adult coughs. Bettye and Sally kept their babies, who were just learning to walk, in freshly polished high-top white shoes, ironed cotton zippered jumpsuits, and carefully buttoned pink and blue sweaters with a row of embroidered ducks on the chest. They immediately dashed into their houses, babies swooped under their arms like shop-lifted food, if they saw a Farmer child *look* as if he or even *thought* about coming close. Farmer children never wore sweaters, coats, or caps. Sally swore once Jill appeared at her door, teeth chattering, bare legs purple as a sparrow's, asking to borrow a cup of sugar. "I sent her home in one of my sweaters," Sally said, "and with a bottle of Stevie's cough syrup and told her to tell her mother the name of the pediatrician on the label."

The kids caused a rash of gossip around the neighborhood—and their coughs a fence of hard feelings between Lottie and Sally-and-Bettye. It seems either Sally or Bettye or both for good measure called the county health department. There was a case of whooping cough in Ashwood Heights. The county nurse could not get out fast enough to investigate. After she left, Lottie went from house to house on three streets, her children clinging to her like possums. "If my children were sick and needed a doctor, I can afford to take them," she said. "They got allergies. Nobody had to go and call the county. My kids got allergies. They ain't nothing contagious."

Another call went to a different county department when

Lottie made the statement she wished she had a cow. Her back yard was big enough for one, there was enough grass, and the fresh milk would better and cheaper for the kids.

"A cow!" Sally rolled her eyes when she heard. "A cow? Out here? Next door?"

Bettye echoed her. Both saw Stevie and Susie in high-top, white polished shoes, stepping, stepping. They had a city official check zoning and restrictions, call Lottie Farmer. Lottie said she never actually planned to get a cow, only that it would be real nice, what with her kids drinking milk like it come from a faucet and all. And prices going up, up, all the time.

Lottie was never included in Sally and Bettye's coffee klatches, but they couldn't help talking to her when they watched their babies in the back yard sandboxes or at the swingset.

No one could ever understand how or why Lottie called on them to act as her private CIA. She must have been desperate and they must have been driven with curiosity. Lottie didn't drive, so either Sally or Bettye drove her and all the kids on her spying missions.

Lottie's husband was called Wink. She pronounced it "Wank" with a long, very flat *a*. Wink drove a city bus. He had a swinging sack of a stomach that must have leaned into the steering wheel and helped pull the tons of bus around curves. His forehead was marked in half by a pale streak from the bill of his cap and he was bald in an oval patch that almost met, but not quite, his pale streak. Lottie giggled a lot when she was around him, said things like "Ain't Wink the cut-up though? Ain't he the stuff?"

What she said to Sally and Bettye when they drove her behind him on his bus route was a different story. Somehow, somewhere, Lottie had gotten wind that Wink had a girl-friend on the side. She wanted to catch him "redhanded," have it out "once and for all."

"Lord, I nearly went crazy," Sally said later. "That bus

stops at every corner and there was Lottie saying every woman who boarded that must be *Her*. 'That's *Her*. I know that's the one.' And the kids were in the back seat fighting or crying over a sucker stick one of them found under the seat."

Finally Lottie hired a taxi for her spying. Where or when she caught Wink no one ever knew—only that she had a moving van to the door and was gone in a day's time. Wink came home to the cleanest house he'd ever seen, walked in, looked around, stood on the porch a few minutes, reached into the outdoor light, unscrewed the bulb, shoved it in his pocket, and left.

A few years later, somebody on Maplewood Lane told Sally, who told Bettye, they had seen Lottie in a nightclub in Atlanta. They said they would never have known her if she hadn't spoken first, introduced herself and her new husband. "He was a good fifteen years younger than Lottie," they said, "and she was dressed up like a doll. Long skirt, eyeshadow, hair dyed dark as night and piled on top of her head like a queen. Nobody in a million years would have known her. She's done all right for herself."

A Second Crop

The house was empty almost a year the second time. Grass, where the Farmer kids had not stamped it out completely, grew in clumps as tall as shrubbery.

Several neighbors snickered it was too bad the Farmers never got that cow.

Everybody complained but nobody did anything, until one day Sally's son brought in a green snake, held out his hand, and said, "Look, Mama." Sally broke a Pyrex dish getting out of the house and over to Bettye's to call Ring, the developer of Ashwood Heights. That afternoon the yard was mowed. Then mercifully it was the hottest, driest August and September on record. Then winter. The stubble was brown, maybe dead, or so Sally hoped.

Next spring, Lottie's yard, everyone still called it that, had weeds high as windows. "Ticks breed in places like that," Bettye said. "And Rocky Mountain spotted fever—there've been two cases reported this year already." She called Ring again. His secretary said the house had been sold and it was up to the new owners to take care of the "grounds."

Six weeks later the new owners moved in. Not during the day, but at night, all night. Several trucks backed in, out, unloaded. Each truck had a bad muffler. And backing seemed to strain both the motors and mufflers, for there was also a lot of yelling. "This way, Charlie. Hold it right there." And odd noises. Toward dawn things got quiet, and Sally said, "I finally closed my eyes and next thing I knew somebody was peeking in my window. He was gone the minute I screamed. I know I didn't dream it . . . and Bob out of town. My God, I was scared out of my mind."

She had to have a third cup of Bettye's good coffee before she could go into the closet to get dressed.

"What kind of people are they?" Sally asked. "With all that noise I expected a circus, tent, elephant, and all."

It took six men with a lawnmower, a scythe, and several rakes to whip the yard into shape.

The Case of the Curious Coathanger

Lisa Miller turned out to be a tall blonde with a fondness for dressing gowns until noon, large diamonds, and a full-time maid. She enjoyed coffee all day and stayed tuned to the latest in gossip. Sally and Bettye took turns entertaining Lisa, defended her when others asked, "What's Lisa Miller with all her diamonds and a maid doing in Ashwood Heights?" Sally said Lisa said it was only until they could find something else. They had to have a place while she looked. Lisa went out looking a lot of afternoons with either Sally or Bettye or both in tow, touring new homes in Rockwall Estates, or Stonebrook Glen. The three decorated for hours over pots of coffee, drew traffic patterns and wall arrangements.

Lisa had to make sure she bought the "right" house. They planned to do quite a bit of entertaining. Her husband's business demanded it. Floy Miller ran a television repair service. "F&S, We Fix the Best, Leave the Rest." Lisa said, one hand holding a cigarette in a teakwood holder, "And you know how much money television people make."

She loved to emphasize that Floy was an independent businessman. The panel trucks and vans with various names and designs spent a lot of trips in and out of the Miller drive. Lisa told Sally that Floy owned ten trucks. They hadn't had time to repaint them; but all the drivers worked *for* him.

"Why are they in and out so much?" Sally asked. She inwardly shuddered at any of the men near six feet tall, remembered the one who had looked in her window that night.

"Floy sends them," Lisa said, "to get things."

"He forgets an awful lot of *things*," Sally told Bettye.

The Millers' Three

Lisa and Floy Miller had three children. A thin, tall gawk of a teenaged boy who wore glasses thick as the bottoms of Coke bottles. Ricky. He smiled when anyone said his name, but was never known to speak a complete sentence. Deena, a five-year-old, was blonde and dimpled. Petula was a dark-haired baby of five months. The maid carried Petula on her hip like a sack most of the time, even home at night. "She's my treasure," Lisa said loudly when the maid was in the room. "My right hand." She also told Sally and Bettye that when Petula was born the doctor found a tumor the size of a grapefruit on her left ovary and one the size of an orange on her right. That she was not supposed to do a thing—not even lift a finger.

When panel trucks and vans were not moving in and out of the Millers' drive, delivery trucks were. Lisa bought a canopy crib for Petula. "This is my last baby and my last chance to get the kind of crib I always wanted for Deena." Sally held her breath at all the eyelet ruffles around the crib's canopy. She said it looked like the one in *Better Homes and Garden*'s May issue. Like a storybook.

Bettye said it would get limp and the first time it was washed would draw up. That it was nothing but a dust-catcher and she wouldn't want one in her house.

Deena's room was painted lavender and Lisa bought layers of lace, ruffles, purple and pink shag carpet. Her lamp was a ballerina who spun on her toes to "Lara's Theme." Then when the light came on she glowed lavender and green.

Bettye said if this house was only temporary, why were they so busy fixing it up?

Sally said the house was so awful Lisa couldn't stand it the way it was another minute. And fixing it up would help the re-sale.

Lisa gave a neighborhood cookout with drinks first at her new upholstered bar in the living room. She had a new, specially made, white sectional sofa, glass tables, and two stereo units, plus plastic plants and hanging baskets. "We're using them for display ideas," Lisa said. "Floy can bring home customers to see how everything looks in actual use. Besides"—she clinked her ring against a glass—"it's tax-deductible."

"So are abortions," Bettye muttered, but only Sally heard her. Lisa had told them she'd done hers herself. Sally, who saw a gynecologist four times a year (five last year, if you counted the time in January she was two days late and panicked) was horrified. She opened her mouth, but no sound came out.

"How?" Bettye asked, her pale eyes large.

"It's easy," Lisa said. "You just take a coathanger, honey. Any kind will do, bend it and—"

"Stop," said Sally. "I can't stand to hear any more. I'm not feeling too well."

The Grand Opening

Lisa earned a red carnation corsage when she became the tenth person to enter the new K-Mart store on Dogwood Boulevard, three blocks south of Ashwood Heights. She also bought one of almost everything in the store. "I opened their first charge account," she said, "and they gave me an umbrella. See." She twirled it around like a flower, tried to tap-dance like Doris Day in *Singing in the Rain.*

"Don't," Bettye said. "That's bad luck."

"I don't believe in it." Lisa kept twirling.

She had also hung so many strands of plastic fruit lanterns across her yard it looked like the hot dog stand at a drive-in movie. She bought shelves for every corner of every room, filled them with china dogs and cats, vases, revolving lights. She cut carpet to fit her bath and bought color-coordinated accessories, plush paper, mat and bowl brush to match. She bought a wading pool for each child—so they wouldn't fuss. Ricky sailed boats in his and tried to drown a couple of cats from the next block. Lisa swore if he got cat scratch fever from the awful claw marks she was going to sue.

"The cats or the owners?" Bettye said from the corner of her mouth.

Lisa made at least one trip a day to K-Mart, sometimes two. She had been known to go three times and once five, if you counted the trip for sno-cones. "I love new things," she said. She especially liked new clothes. She wore things once, gave them to the maid. Ricky's, Deena's, and Petula's too.

Floy wore gray uniforms the maid washed and ironed. His name was embroidered in red thread above the front pocket and "F&S" across the back.

"Does Floy Miller make that kind of money?" Bettye asked. Floy was an angry man who chewed stumpy cigars, slammed doors on trucks, cars, and houses, raced motors, and cussed in what Bettye said sounded like an original language.

"He has to be in something illegal," Bettye's husband said. "Nobody makes TV house calls at 2:00 a.m."

The K-Mart Kid

Ricky tried to hold not only the neighborhood cats underwater but also Stevie, Sally's son. "Ricky had been so sweet to come over, offer to watch Stevie, to share his pool . . . I tried to think I didn't see what I saw from my kitchen window. Thank God I ran out in time."

The next time Lisa told the story of Ricky's brilliant school career and how the teacher sent him home because he was two grades ahead of the other children and "there was nothing she could teach him," Sally excused herself from the room.

According to Lisa, Ricky had read every book in the county they moved from and the librarian just adored him.

Bettye cleared her throat at that, looked out the window, made another pot of coffee.

When Lisa rang their doorbells one night at 2:35 a.m., asking if they'd seen Ricky, neither got upset nor went with her to call the police nor drive around Ashwood Heights looking for him. "Where's Floy?" Sally said. "Maybe Ricky's with him." She went back to bed and woke up with a migraine.

Lisa had three police cars in her drive the next morning. They stayed until noon. Ricky had been found at K-Mart.

He'd gone to buy a goldfish for his pool and waited all night for the store to open. He slept in the Ride-Um Rocket and nobody saw him until some kid came up to ride and Ricky wouldn't let him in.

Several people from the Juvenile Authorities inquired around the neighborhood. Sally assured them Lisa was an excellent mother and Ricky an unusual child.

Bettye said there was something funny going on over there and she didn't know if it was all legal and not to mention her name in connection with anything.

Lisa started helping Floy "at the office." She left every morning before seven in a green Plymouth that was ten years old and had four dented fenders with rusty holes like lace. She didn't get in until after ten at night.

Ricky was sent to a special school in another state—or that's what Lisa told someone. Deena went to live with her grandparents in Florida and the maid took Petula. Floy told Sam, Sally's husband, that Petula was not his child and never had been.

Several months passed and no one entered the Miller house. Floy saw Sam once in the bowling alley and said that Lisa had left him for a keyboard player and was living in Nashville, if you could call that living. He didn't. That he was doing fine and had a cot in the back of his shop, took all his meals out.

Sally and Sam were transferred to Dallas. Bettye gave her a going-away coffee. She polished the silver service she had saved thirty-two books of stamps for four years to get. She baked a carrot cake and bought some green mints from the drugstore and said if that wasn't good enough for Miss Got-rocks, she didn't care. She didn't keep Sally's baby while she packed, nor waved when the van left, nor get her forwarding address.

She told her husband that she hoped the real estate agent was a decent one and would be picky about who he showed the house to.

Meanwhile she planted a hedge of thorny limes, put in a birdbath, bought two pink plastic flamingos, and ordered a flagpole. At an auction she bought a black iron washpot, had it hauled home, and planted it by her front door. By June, purple-striped petunias tumbled their heads out.

The Miller house was emptied. Mostly by creditors. One took the furniture, another the stereo stuff. Others came to Bettye's door asking questions. "I only met them a few times," she said. "I don't know anything."

Two empty houses in the middle of the street affected the entire neighborhood, Bettye thought. They looked like cast-off clothes, faded, scruffy, weak at the seams.

She and several others complained to Ring, the developer. Then they passed around a petition and got sixty-three signatures. Ring took over the Miller house, painted, wallpapered, glassed in the back porch, seeded and landscaped the yard. He hired a decorator who made it into a "Model Home for the Modest Budget," and it was featured in full color on the front of the Sunday newspaper. Bettye burned. The nerve of him. Making the rest of them look like fools with his money.

The house sold to a retired couple from Newark who planned to put a greenhouse in the back yard. They also announced they didn't like children and preferred privacy.

Sally's house sold to blacks. Bettye and her husband panicked, put a sign out overnight. They took a five-thousand-dollar loss and said they were lucky at that, in trade for a split-level in Merry Hope Run.

Martha White, the black who bought Sally's place, became block chairman for the first neighborhood picnic. The streets were blocked off, everyone brought a covered dish, and there was music and dancing, beer and wine until the wee hours.

Someone said they thought they saw Floy Miller dancing with Lottie Farmer, but no one could be sure. It was that kind of party.

The Blue Bonnet Bug

THE SOUND WAKES me. Someone is opening gifts. Opening and opening and opening. It seems like the middle of night or just before dawn. I think the tissue paper will never stop. They will never get to the gift. Hurry. I am pulling at the sheet, wadding the blanket. It is dark and I can't think where there is tissue in my bedroom. The sounds come from the closet. Someone is opening gifts in my closet?

I nudge Brian. "Listen."

"Huh?" He wakes slow, mud-headed.

I nudge harder, this time with my knee.

"Huh, huh, huh . . . what is it?" He half wakes, lifts his leaden head. I see the fine line of his chin in the dark.

"Listen."

"I don't hear anything."

"In the closet. Listen."

He listens. I see his forehead concentrate.

"Mice," he says disgustedly, pounds his pillow, sinks back to sleep.

I lie rigid. Awake in every cell. Scared. *Mice.* Mice are almost rats and the last time I knew rats I was five, Mother and I alone in a rented house. "It's all I could find," she says. We live in two rooms. Another family on the other side. A wide, dark hall between us. I hear people knock on their door. Voices. Cabbage and onion odors. Voices. I ride a school bus to a building crowded with strangers. At night I listen to the cream-colored radio on the table in our kitchen, my face warm against the tubes and lights. Ozzie and Harriet, Jack Benny, Dagwood and Blondie.

At night Mother and I hear feet overhead. Hundreds of feet, running, thumping, jumping. A parade, a city, an upper world. "Rats," Mother says, and holds me close. "They won't come down here." I wondered how she knew, how she could be sure. I saw one rat in the yard once. He was large as a cat, with hard, bright eyes and teeth sharp as a trap. The rat glowered at me, parted the weeds and left like a shot.

Mother bought traps, baited them with gold cubes of the cheese I loved. "Don't dare touch them," she said. "Rats carry diseases."

"What kind?" I asked, thinking of measles and chicken pox.

"The bubonic plague," she said.

I shuddered.

She sets traps carefully around the rooms. I am afraid to walk at night, to go to the bathroom, lie holding myself full and hot. Sometimes in the dark I hear traps click in loud, red whacks. In the mornings, they are always empty. No rats, no cheese.

"I'm only feeding the things," Mother said.

We find small black curds in our kitchen drawers, in our underwear. Mother scrubs things, boils them, cleans, shakes things, cries. I cry. Rats, awful rats.

We keep writing letters to my father. At last he comes. Mother runs to him, ducks her face into his arms. His sleeve in a uniform the color of dead grass scratches my face. Buttons brush my cheek as he lifts me up. "It's terrible," Mother says. "We have *rats.*"

My father helps us get our things. We move to a hotel until he leaves. Then we ride a bus to my grandmother's in Mississippi, her clean house with curtains and starch and quiet ceilings.

Brian and I have quiet ceilings. They peak to a point with glass and overlook a lake, meadow and fields beyond. There are houses on each side of us, on the other streets, with more to be built on the meadow across the lake.

"Mice are not rats," Brian says at breakfast. He pours milk over cereal. "These are tiny field mice. They won't hurt you."

At work, I tell Ellie about the mice. "I can't sleep."

She stops opening mail, letter knife in her hand. "What you need is Amanda."

"Is she a mouser?" I wonder that Mother never thought of a cat. A cat would have been so much nicer than gray, flapping traps and disease all around.

I stop by Ellie's after work, bring Amanda home. In her travel cage she rides like a trapped beast, a yellow tiger. She howls, she paces, she is my protector. O Amanda—I stroke her through the bars—we will slay the mice.

Amanda, out of the cage, backs into the corner with the ficus. I catch and carry her to the bedroom, petting and talking all the way. She sniffs the closet, shoots back to the living room.

"Don't let the cat out," I yell. Brian blocks the door with the mail, his briefcase.

"What cat?"

Amanda slides between his legs. I dash after. "Amanda!" A yellow blur flicks through the hedge. "Kitty, kitty, here kitty."

I run six blocks, through yards, around fences, across budding border beds. I am wild in my chase—and unfruitful.

Later Brian drives the car and I call with cupped hands,

"Amanda, here kitty."

What to tell Ellie? She's had the cat nine years, feeds her only the best. I should never have borrowed her. Never brought her home. Is she so afraid of mice that even the scent sent her running?

I wait until after dinner, hope against hope that somehow Amanda will reappear. Decide to return to her job, help me with my battle.

At nine-thirty, Ellie calls. "What happened? I heard a scratch at the door and there rubbed Amanda."

The cat has traveled several miles and some super-expressways. How in the world—? Fear can do strange things. Now that Amanda is safe I scoff. Coward.

Brian discovers how the mice have gotten in the house. A large opening around the water cutoff in my closet. Whoever put a water cutoff in a closet?

"At least we know where it is," Brian says. He finds a board and nails it tight. No more mice. Ah Brian, my protector. Who needs a cat?

It is wonderful in bed and I sleep until sometime in the almost light I hear the gift opening again. "Mice!"

I wake Brian.

"We must have trapped them in the house. They can't get back out."

At lunch I buy three mousetraps in a hardware store that smells of oil and sawdust and seeds. Traps with metal clamps and little clickety, gossipy tongues. They rattle, tattle in the bag as I walk to work, lie in my desk drawer like accusations.

After dinner Brian plays with them, hooking nutmeats, perfect pecan and walnut halves, into place. I argue for cheese and we settle for baiting one with cheese, two with nuts.

I carry the set traps as carefully as decorated hors d'oeuvres, to the bedroom, hall, kitchen.

Sometime in the night, I hear a clack, a whap, a final

whamp. I snuggle closer to Brian. There are no screams. No mice death protests. All is quiet. I am a contented coward in the dark, dreaming of blackberry thickets and picking with my mother. Briars pull me, tangles of wire and bare feet. I wake thirsty, dry-throated.

Before Brian is up, I swirl into a robe and check my traps. String of a tail, finger of fur, one small, gray mouse. His tiny teeth stopped on the cheese. He *is* small. Not like a rat at all, but some novelty for a key chain, a woodland creature with a mushroom for an umbrella, a caricature for a child's picture book. And I killed him. Very dead. I feel terrible, have an urge I ought to send flowers, hang a wreath. In Miceville are they passing the news? John is gone. Martha a widow. Are there five mouse children made fatherless? I lean closer and touch him with my bare toe. He is soft, still, and so very small. I touch him again.

"You did it." Brian clamps a warm hand on my shoulder. I jump.

"You caught him." He looks at my mouse as if it were a trophy. A beast I have bagged ready to be stuffed and mounted. I see a row of them for my wall, a den of conquests.

In the hall we find the second dead mouse, quiet in his trap. And in the kitchen is a third. I pull my robe tighter, walk a half-circle to the sink.

"Take them out," I tell Brian.

"Not me." He makes toast, goes to the cabinet for grape jelly. "I didn't do it."

"Please." I'm clutching the edge of the counter now.

He eats his toast at the table like a small boy, gets jelly on his cheek.

How can he eat with a house full of dead mice?

"They didn't bother me alive," he says, brushing crumbs into his hand. "No big deal . . . couple of mice."

He goes to shower and I watch him carefully walk far around the mouse. As though *he* is afraid of it. I hear him whistling in the hall, bedroom, until he is past and the noise of his razor comforts him.

He was afraid and wouldn't admit it. Big hero, big protector. Big deal. And now he's afraid to empty the traps.

I grab a wastebasket and scoop the kitchen mouse and trap into it, then the hall one, then my poor dead Johnny Mouse. They tumble in the crumpled papers, lie there as if they are covered with flowers.

I clamp on the lid and dash to the house, wash my hands in hottest water, shower until my skin tingles almost raw. Then hum as I dress. Ha, Brian, ha. I know your secret, you big, cool fake. Afraid of mice. I touched one!

At the office, Ellie and I swim through end-of-the-month reports. We come up long enough for some soup and a salad brought in at three. At four I feel feverish, nauseated, chilled. Probably a touch of something, Ellie says. I know different. It is the bubonic plague. The blue bonnet disease, I used to call it. It strikes fast. In my mind I hear Mother's voice saying, "It killed thousands." Big, brave, foolish me—touching the mouse.

Ellie offers to finish up if I want to go home.

I cower on the living room sofa, bundled in a white afghan my grandmother crocheted. Shells and ripples that make me dizzy but warm.

Brian lets himself in, sees me and is surprised. He feels my forehead. "No fever."

"I have chills."

He takes my temperature. Normal. These are the chills before the fever, I know that. Warnings, before the real stuff sets in.

Brian tucks the afghan in tight around me, kisses the top of my head. He brings me hot tea and toast on a tray, builds a fire in the fireplace. Feeling much better, I slide the afghan down and stretch.

Brian rubs my feet with his hands, kisses one of my ankles. "It was probably just a touch of a bug," he says.

"Yes," I murmur, "I'm sure that's what it was."

Judas at the Table

MAREN NEVER KNOWS how many she'll have for Thanksgiving dinner until they walk through the door, but she isn't worried. It's covered-dish, and covered-dish always works out. There are always leftovers. The Asheville part of the Deal family has written they're bringing ham. Maren could have predicted that. Aunt Stella brings the turkey. Each year she worries, will it be tender? Will it be dry? It is never either, but she worries. Maren's mother calls to say she'll bring cranberry salad, sweet potatoes, pumpkin pie. It wouldn't be Thanksgiving without pumpkin pie. Maren hates it. Her two brothers and their current wives are coming. Then Ted's father, Frank; his brother, Tommy; and Tommy's wife, Lynda. With Ted and Maren, that makes thirteen, but who's counting? She doesn't set the table until everyone arrives.

Out-of-towners arrive first: Uncle Al and Aunt Lillian, the Asheville Deals, at the touch of twelve. Maren meets them at the car. Ted is still in the shower. He raked leaves until fifteen minutes ago—a job Maren has asked him to do for the last two weeks.

"Here you are," Aunt Lillian says. "Look at you." Aunt Lillian was a family therapist until she retired five years ago.

Uncle Al is retired from the post office. "How's my favorite niece?"

Maren kisses his cool cheek, which smells faintly lime. "Your only niece," she says, "but I'm glad you like me."

"You wouldn't be my favorite if I didn't." He laughs, takes off a brown pancake of a cap. He's seventy, Maren thought, and his hair dark as ever. Maybe darker. He touches it up, she's sure, but that's okay. Aunt Lillian told her once how they'd met. During the war, at a USO dance. "I saw him across the room and thought he was the handsomest man I'd ever seen." She paused, then added in a softer tone, "I still do." Cornell Wilde, Maren thought. Yes, that's who her uncle looked like. She remembered a huge picture of Cornell Wilde that hung in the lobby of a local theater when she was growing up. Then forty-nine years into their marriage, Maren heard the story, realized who her uncle looks like.

She hugs her aunt, who is powdery and light. Maren smells mothballs and can't imagine why. Aunt Lillian has dressed entirely in black the last twenty years, ever since the double mastectomy. Today she wears a black pantsuit, black blouse with tiny sprigs of red. She carries the ham from the car, her shoulder bag, but no Thermos. Maren looks for the Thermos. Aunt Lillian never goes anywhere without coffee, not even to another room. It's been the family joke as long as Maren can remember that Aunt Lillian is a "coffee head," a "coffee junkie." Today she has only the ham rocking in its dish, spilling juices down her leg.

"It's wonderful to see you." Maren carries a cake in its see-through plastic keeper. "You made this?"

"With a little help from Sara Lee." Aunt Lillian grins.

"I've never known a Thanksgiving to be so warm," says Uncle Al. He wears a tan windbreaker. "There's snow in the

Midwest. They can have it."

"We'll all be sick," Aunt Stella says. She arrived with Maren's mother and "the bird," twenty pounds of brown that glows on a tray like it's been waxed. The picture of Thanksgiving. "Look at this bird," she says. Aunt Stella is a gray wisp of a woman who never married and is proud of it. "I had my chances," she likes to say, "and made my choices. I never missed a thing." She wears a red bow in her hair that matches her lace-trimmed apron.

Maren has been up since six. She made a broccoli casserole, creamed onions, and a brandied pound cake. She feels slightly damp, hot, and tired. Wilted. She spent time on a fresh flower centerpiece and candles, but is waiting to set the table. Last night she polished the silver. Last night after Kellie called. "Mama, I'm not coming home," she said. "There's a bunch of kids here and we're going to Connecticut to ski. You don't mind, do you?"

Mind? Of course Maren minds. She minds a hell of a lot.

"It's only two weeks until Christmas vacation and I'll be home then," Kellie said. "It's silly to come home for only the weekend."

Sure, Maren thought. Sure, the whole Thanksgiving thing is silly to you. Family is silly. Parents are silly. Parents who spend themselves silly to send you to that fancy school because you failed two others.

"What's this?" Maren's brother Jim says, hands on her waist, lifting her a little. "One of those Pick-Me-Up Bouquets?"

"No," she says. "It's one of those I-Made-It-Myself in the green tissue from Food World." Jim and Susie have just arrived with a casserole and her cat, Toot, an overgrown gray tabby with a red rhinestone collar. Toot immediately fled under the living room sofa. "She'll come out when she smells the turkey," Susie says. "And that's when we'll have to watch her."

"It's lovely," Aunt Lillian says.

Does she mean the table or the cat or Jim and Susie? Maren wonders. Aunt Lillian calls Jim by his brother's name and she's given up on wives. That's what she said last year. She can't keep track of these on-again-off-again new kinds of marriages. She pulls open an end-table drawer, muttering. The drawer is where Maren keeps the only ashtray in the house. Aunt Lillian shuts the drawer as though she suddenly realizes she doesn't need it. This is one of the few times Maren has seen her aunt without a cup of coffee or cigarette in her hands, or both. However, lately, her aunt has been taking her cigarettes outside to smoke, saying, "No one can say I inflict my bad habits on them." So this is "cold turkey," Maren thinks, and not like Lillian at all. She looks strained, her wrinkles deeper, complexion paler, almost transparent. And this time she didn't get her hair rinse right. Instead of the usual auburn, she got bright pink in places. Cotton candy pink. Lillian wanders around the table muttering, as though looking for a cigarette or match . . . something. Anything.

Meanwhile, in the kitchen, Aunt Stella and Maren's mother have the casseroles under control, rolls out of wrappers, gravy and dressing warming in the microwave.

Maren counts placemats. With Tommy and Lynda there will be thirteen. She gets out napkins, silver. There's space for twelve at the table with the leaves in. She sets another place at once end. That makes thirteen. She lights the candles, stands back. The table does look good and Maren doesn't feel so tired for a minute.

Tommy and Lynda arrive last, bringing Ted's father, Frank. Widowed a year ago, Frank still seems dazed, lost, a little confused. Lynda carries a little girl of about two, who hugs a blue Care Bear.

"Oh," Aunt Lillian says, "you got it already."

"No, no," says Lynda, "she isn't ours. We don't have ours yet. This is Stacy. Her mama's a friend and I said I'd take her for the day." Stacy has hair the color of frost and eyes blue as plastic.

"Set another place," Aunt Stella hisses to Maren, wiping her hands on her red apron. "I'm so relieved we have another person. Thank goodness." Before Maren can get another placemat, Aunt Stella has pulled one from the drawer, laid it on the table. "Thank goodness," she says, and rushes back to the kitchen.

"She can eat at the counter," Lynda says. "Put a place here."

"No, no," says Aunt Stella. "I've already got it set and you just leave it. Bring a kitchen stool for her."

Maren has fixed iced tea. If anyone wants anything else right now she's not offering it. Tea now, coffee later, except she hasn't made coffee yet. She made tea with the coffee-maker and you can't do both at the same time. She can't believe Aunt Lillian has been in the house longer than thirty minutes and not had a cup of coffee. She isn't Aunt Lillian without coffee and cigarettes.

Uncle Al carves the turkey, white and dark meat piling evenly in layers on the platter.

"I hope it's tender." Aunt Stella hovers at his elbow. "I hope it's not dry."

"It's tender," says Uncle Al. "Falling off the knife. I could have cut it with a string."

Ted tastes a piece. "If it was any more tender, we'd have to eat it with a spoon." He has grumbled so much about doing anything in the yard lately that Maren is ready to sell the 3,500 square feet on eight acres and buy a condo in town. Something with a concrete yard. How would he like that? The eight acres are woods and he couldn't get enough of them when they bought out here fifteen years ago. A year after they were married and Kellie a baby. There were no neighbors for miles. If Maren hadn't gone to work in Kellie's school as the secretary she would have lost her mind. Ted only has to mow or rake a postage stamp–sized strip around the house. It doesn't take him half an hour, but he growls for hours before and weeks afterwards. Maren is tired of his attitude lately. His attitude toward everything.

Frank says the blessing. He's fast and mumbles through "Thankyouforwhatweareabouttoreceiveandblessusaswego-throughthecomingyearamen." They file past the buffet, filling plates, stacking rolls atop servings of casserole, salad, sweet potatoes. "I hope the turkey's good," Aunt Stella says.

"All this good food," says Aunt Lillian, "and it goes right to my hips. I've got to quit. Just quit." Lillian always diets, eats carrot strips like popcorn, lives on celery, and seems to look always the same. Not thin, not chubby, somewhere in between. "Long ago I quit telling people what to do," she says, forking a cranberry. Lillian still has a small home practice in family therapy, with a dozen or so patients. "But sometimes I have to comment."

"You can comment," Maren teases. "We'll let you."

"Just this strange thing. Our good friend, Lewis Gormon, died. You met the Gormons."

Maren remembers them. They've been Al and Lillian's neighbors for forty years. In fact the whole neighborhood is people who've been there forty years or so. Lillian has described it as the "next thing to a retirement village with the only difference being they all own their own homes and have lived there forever."

"Lew died last week," Aunt Lillian continues, "and they had the strangest service. No funeral. Just a memorial." She shakes her head. "Six people stood up and talked about Lew. Even death isn't sacred any more."

Maren says, "It sounds very contemporary to me. Did you see *The Big Chill*?" Then realizes her aunt and uncle don't go to movies, don't get HBO. In fact they don't go out at night at all. Or any place they can help it. Today is a rare visit.

"It was awful," Aunt Lillian shudders. "The son spoke of going into bars with his father, taking him home after. Only the daughter gave a touching tribute."

"Did they say anything that wasn't true?" Ted asks.

"No," Lillian says.

"Anything you didn't know already?"

She shakes her head, doesn't seem to be listening. "The only thing they didn't mention was other women. They spared us that, thank goodness."

"But you all knew?" Maren asks.

"Yes, everybody knew."

"So it's okay to know something as long as nobody talks about it openly, honestly. Is that it?" Ted says.

"It's the way the whole thing was done." Lillian seems far away, not eating now, but moving food around in circles on her plate. "I still can't get over it. I'm sorry I went."

At the other end of the table, Aunt Stella is talking of Lisa. "She's separated."

"When?" Lillian asks. "When did this happen?"

Lisa is a cousin, daughter of Al and Stella's oldest sister, Sally.

"Quite a while ago." Stella holds her mouth in a firm, disapproving line. "They just didn't tell it. Not after all that wedding and Sally bragging what a good catch he was."

"Well, I want my twenty-five dollars back." Lillian lifts herself a slice of lemon chess pie from the plate being passed. "Does anyone know why?" She takes a slice of pecan now, then chocolate meringue.

"Money," says Stella. "That's all he thought about. She said they always had good communications. The whole time. They never had trouble with that. Just money. He couldn't get enough."

Lillian sighs. "Long-term marriages are a matter of luck. I came to that conclusion a long time ago."

Before Maren can say what she has on the tip of her mind, Uncle Al says, "Did I ever tell you about the Deal who signed the Declaration of Independence? He was the one who raised the money for Washington's troops to cross the Delaware."

Maren laughs. "The Deals could do it. We got the

whatever-it-takes-to-get-the-job-done." She adds that she ought to trace the Deals back so she could join the DAR. "It might be fun."

Her brother Jim, loaded spoonful of banana pudding paused on the way to his mouth, says, "Maren, next thing you know, you'll be tracing us back to the NAACP."

Everyone at the table laughs and Maren pokes her tongue at him.

"Papa said once," Uncle Al continues, "some people from Philadelphia came to see him trying to trace Deals about an inheritance. If we could have proved our line direct, we could have inherited a lot of money. But we never could. Courthouse in Union burned and all the records with it."

"Makes it awfully convenient," Ted says, and Maren knees him under the table.

"A lot of courthouses in the South burned," she says.

"Deals are something else," Lillian says. "Al isn't manic-depressive, paranoid, schizophrenic, any of the above. And my family has it all. We divided it up evenly among us."

"The Deals were too poor," says Maren. "All they had was farms and hard work staring them in the face. They didn't have time to be neurotic."

"When we got married," Uncle Al says, "I told Lillian there was going to be some stepping on toes. She was going to step on mine and I was going to step on hers."

"And you have," Aunt Lillian says quickly. She looks around as if a cigarette is going to descend upon her from the air.

"You know what happens when toes get stepped on? They get sore. And when a sore toe gets stepped on too much, you yell. So I say you better yell before your toes get sore."

"Communicate," Maren says, and looks at Ted, who is eating more turkey, dressing, gravy. "You had the answer before all the marriage counselors. Fifty years before."

Aunt Lillian gives her a gray little look. "Long-term marriages are a matter of luck—pure and simple."

"No," says Maren. "It's not that simple. You can't call it chance, like a card game. It's damn hard work."

Ted takes his plate and tea glass, goes to the kitchen.

The child Tommy and Lynda brought has ringed her plate with food, eaten little. Now she pats her marshmallow salad with the back of her spoon. "I'm going to bash somebody's head in," she says loudly to everybody and nobody. "I'm going to take my spoon and bash some heads in."

Lynda takes Stacy's spoon from her, puts food back in her plate. "I'll be glad when we get ours." She doesn't look at Stacy or anyone. Only the table. "I can't wait."

"I'm so glad you brought her," Aunt Stella says. "Thirteen at the table is bad luck. Haven't you always heard that? I've heard it all my life. Some people won't eat at a table if there's thirteen. They take their plate and go someplace else."

"Why?" Maren asks. She's never heard this before.

"Judas," Stella says. "Nobody wants to be Judas."

Even the Bees in Denmark

LATER HE WOULD talk at great length about the nude beaches and she never added to it, never interrupted, only smiled and held in her mind a scene he missed, he'd never know because she'd never tell him. Talk about the nude beaches was a sure attention-getter and he gloried in the risqué spotlight he created for himself among friends, family, delighting when their Baptist faces dropped, their Methodist minds fastened on him. "A car would pull up," he'd say, "and the whole family would jump out stark naked. Not a stitch among them. They'd make a mad dash for the water." He told of badminton games played on the Danish beaches, all players naked. Bridge games on blankets, each hand-held by men and women in the buff. "No one thought anything about it," he'd add, "like it was the normal way to be."

He'd watch looks on faces and when he saw the question blossoming, he'd head it off. "Of course, we weren't nude. We wore bathing suits—such as they were—borrowed from our friends. But we changed behind the dunes. I tell you that was really something." He'd poke an elbow in her ribs. That was what she remembered. That he elbowed her every time they saw someone nude. At least he hadn't embarrassed her then. He hadn't said anything in front of the Jorgensens. Frankly it wasn't that big a deal. Everyone seemed to be enjoying the beach, acted so absolutely normal, she forgot most of them wore no clothes. She did remember noticing one heavily bearded bald fellow who strolled along with only a towel hung over his shoulders. He smoked the biggest cigar she'd ever seen. In fact it was bigger than anything else he carried.

She remembered the fine, white sand on the dunes. How it dusted off like sugar. They used the dunes for shelter from the sharp wind, had coffee and pastries with chocolate. They drove leisurely back and she loved the countryside, cows, fields of blooming heather, wildflowers. Curt Jorgensen even stopped to let her pick wildflowers. She thumped a fat, lazy bee off one purple flower. They laughed the bee hadn't protested, merely droned on to the next flower. "Even the bees are happy in Denmark," Curt said. Kristen translated for them and they batted the phrase around in various ways in the days that followed.

A week later they were in Copenhagen and she still had jet lag. She'd wake at 2:00 a.m., unable to go back to sleep, then was terribly tired in the afternoons. Several times she got up, sat on the patio or in the garden, and waited for the rest of the world to awake. He didn't like her to do that. Didn't like to wake up and find her bed empty. Couldn't understand what bothered her, why she couldn't sleep at night, wanted to nap in the afternoons. There were things to do in the afternoons, places to go, museums, shops, tours. They had only three days left. She could nap at home. He didn't care, but for God's sake, while they were here, he sure as hell wanted to get his money's worth. Everything wasn't exactly cheap over here no matter where the dollar was and the rate of exchange. She got so tired trying to figure out kroner, dollars and cents. He carried the calculator, got annoyed if she asked to use it. Next time she'd bring her own. Next time. Already she wanted to come back. There was too much and she missed the one thing she really wanted to see, the Little Mermaid.

"It's not on the beaten track," he said. "It's out in the harbor and it's not all that big. You'll be disappointed after you see it."

She didn't care. It was the idea. She'd grown up on Hans Christian Andersen's stories, almost memorized them at one point in her life.

"You've seen the museum, his bedroom—all that junk. It was nothing but a bookstore. Weren't you disappointed?" he badgered. "Tell me the truth."

"I wasn't disappointed. It doesn't matter his birthplace was turned into a museum and bookstore. I liked just being there."

"Was the ground holy or something?" he said.

"Maybe. Something like that." It wasn't what he wanted to hear and she did really want to see the Little Mermaid.

"You'd have to take a tour and that's expensive," he said.

"Not that expensive. We could check."

"It would take time and we don't have that."

True. They had narrowed down museums and castles to ones close that could be done in a day or half-day. The castle outside Copenhagen was where his camera jammed and he spent an hour in the courtyard cussing, trying to pry it open. She told him they could go to a camera shop. There had to be a number of them around and someone would speak English, she was sure. He said the camera had jammed before. He'd always fixed it. He'd fix it now if he could get to a darkroom.

"A camera shop would have one," she said. "Let's find one."

"They'll ruin the film," he said. "I'll do it myself. I've done it before. Besides, they'd charge you an arm and a leg."

He refused to buy slides, saying he'd fix the camera, they'd come back in the afternoon. Their tickets were good all day. There were things he wanted pictures of, too.

She slept on the grass alongside the moat. For an hour. A delicious hour in sun the color of marigolds. She slept on the all-weather coat he insisted they carry. They hadn't seen rain in almost two weeks, but the guidebooks said all-weather coats were essential.

When she woke in the shadow of the castle, the castle with spires like lances, he was not in sight. She stretched, felt wonderful. Funny how she couldn't shake what the light did to her. She knew now why Danes love sun. Before she left the States, a friend had taken her aside, said, "Don't be surprised at anything you see in Denmark." Lucy waited, wondered what she meant. "I just want you to be prepared," Ann had said.

"For what?" Lucy asked.

"Danes love the sun," Ann said. "Don't be surprised if you see someone sitting on a park bench suddenly remove her blouse, sit there bare-breasted soaking up the sun."

Lucy laughed, thanked Ann. Was that all? The idea didn't bother Lucy a bit. If someone wanted to take off everything and sit in the sun awhile it was okay with Lucy. She didn't think she'd do it but there was nothing wrong with what someone else chose to do. After her nap on the grass, Lucy understood. She would have removed her blouse if she could capture and keep some of that sun. That and the grass, her nap, made her feel like a child, rested, warm, and hungry. They'd missed lunch. The castle tearoom closed while he was working on his camera.

He came now from the other side of a black marble statue of a pawing, prancing, nostril-snorting bull. She hadn't seen it before.

"Did you think I'd left you?" he said, broken camera still on a strap around his neck. "Serve you right if I did. Let you find your way back by yourself."

She resolved to start dropping mental breadcrumbs, marking directions. Somehow it didn't bother her. She'd ask until she found someone who spoke English.

It made him angry when he had to check his camera with the guard at the Royal Doulton showrooms. It wasn't one of the places he'd wanted to visit, but there it was on the main street, and she was inside before he realized where they were. She sank in carpet almost to her knees and was dazzled by displays of glass and mirrors. When the uniformed guard stepped forward to take his camera, Allen stepped back, held it close, started to leave.

"It's policy," she said. "For goodness' sakes let him have it."

"It's an expensive camera," Allen said.

"So," she said, "and broken. Maybe he can fix it."

"Ha," Allen said.

She wanted to buy something, anything, here. "I love this place," she said. They watched women in identical blue and white smocks paint flesh-colored plates, cups, bowls. He tugged her away, but they had to go through the salesroom to reach the elevator. She lingered with plaques of the four seasons, bisque, bas-relief. "You'll break it," he said. "You don't have room in your suitcase."

"I'll carry it," she said, and settled on "Night," which showed an angel with a child under each arm, owls and bats overhead.

"It's too expensive," he said. "Maybe you'll see it someplace else cheaper."

"No," she said, "this is the factory. It's cheaper here."

"You don't know when we'll get to a bank."

"We haven't touched the traveler's checks." She hugged her plaque.

"You don't know how much it will cost to fix the camera."

"We'll put it on credit cards."

"You don't know that," he said. "You can't Visa every-where in the world no matter what you think."

She figured out the exchange rate, didn't ask for the calcu-lator. Twenty-eight dollars. The plaque would be triple that at home. She'd never buy it at home. Here, she wanted it with all her heart. In the end she charged it. Of course they had Visa. They were delighted to charge it.

He didn't say a word. The traveler's checks were still untouched. They'd be home in three days. For two weeks he had worried about every cent they spent. He was still doing it. To make her miserable? Frighten her? She'd be penniless in a foreign country. She was sure there would be Traveler's Aid, an embassy; they could borrow from the Sorensens.

There was a restaurant through double glass doors, tables under white umbrellas in a garden beside a wall where water spilled down, splashed musically below. Geraniums and im-patiens tumbled in pinks, reds, whites from every available container. It looked delightful. She opened the doors, smelled water, coffee, and the warm wafts of something crisp and sugary baking.

"Wait." He pulled her back. "This place will charge three prices for everything."

"How much can coffee cost?" she said. "For goodness' sakes?"

They hadn't had lunch and she was starved. "I'll check the menu and if it's too much, we'll just get coffee."

"I'm hungry and I don't want to waste my time and my money on an expensive cup of coffee. There are other places. Let's go."

They reclaimed the camera. "Didn't fix it," he mumbled, and pointed out what he said was a new scratch on the case.

She didn't know how he could tell. He'd had the camera five years, she knew. The case was already worn. It was the worst-looking camera the guard took from a row of them beside the entrance. She almost laughed, instead cradled her package close, followed him out.

She thought they walked forever and still hadn't found a shop where he would eat. Her feet felt heavy and numb. Like bricks, except bricks didn't have blisters and she was sure she had blisters.

Finally, one shop had nothing but pastries and breads in their window. Every shape, every size. Every price probably, she thought.

"Isn't this better?" Allen said. "You can see what you're getting. Pick what you want."

The shop was packed with people. She tried to read the prices—.5 and .7, 1.5—and stay in line. Finally she pointed to a torte delicate as lace, rich in chocolate and creams as truffles, and looked for the cashier. Her pastry was passed down a line like a cafeteria toward a beverages worker. Allen chose something that looked greasy, stale, like a flat dough-nut. Lucy hoped it would be good.

"I want something cold to drink," he said. "Order a soda for me."

"I can't," she said. "I don't know the word."

"Order it," he said.

"You order it," she called over her shoulder as the line of people surged forward.

"You're first in line. Order for both of us."

When the line moved past the woman catching cups of coffee from a steaming urn, calling, *"Kafe? Kafe?* You like *kafe?"*

Lucy hesitated, said, "Soda. Cold soda."

"Kafe?" the woman chanted. *"Kafe?"* She pushed a cup onto the tray with Lucy's torte. *"Kafe?"* She pointed to Al-len, ran another steaming cup, rocked it on the tray. *"Kafe?"* she said to the next person. *"Kafe?"*

The small space was packed with tables, people, shopping bags. Lucy eased her way between them, toward the one empty table in the back corner, put her tray down. Her knees felt weak and she had a dull throb in both temples.

"I didn't want coffee," Allen said, gritted his teeth. "I told you I didn't want coffee." He had sloshed his into the saucer, onto the tray. "I wanted a soft drink. Soda. I would have taken any kind. Anything cold."

Their table was beneath a mural. A faded garden painted onto the wall, like a window with a view instead of a flat wall. It was effective from a distance. Lucy had thought at first glance the shop opened onto a small walled garden.

She brushed crumbs from the last patron into her hand, dusted them into the ashtray full of twisted brown cigarettes. Her coffee was too hot to drink. Much too hot. Steam circled and swirled, rose like a genie. How did they get coffee so hot in this country?

The whole place was too warm, sugary smelling, air heavy as syrup. The kind of place bees would gather. In fact there was a buzz about the room—the hum and buzz of blended conversations, and none of them in English. Lucy listened, felt strange.

Allen pushed his pastry aside. "It's stale," he said. "And this damn coffee. I told you I wanted soda."

"Why didn't you tell the waitress?" she said. Her pastry was wonderful, rich, creamy . . . everything it looked. She took tiny bites, let them melt on her tongue. The torte had whipped cream, hazelnuts, a slight rum flavor.

"Why don't you get another pastry?" she said. "Get one of these. It's really good. Want a taste?"

"It looks gooey," he said, "and I'm not about to get back in that line. I'd be crushed."

"You could try to get a soda."

"I asked you to get me a soda," he said, "the first time. That's what I wanted."

"I tried," she said.

"You didn't try very hard." His words had edges sharp as knives. "You don't give a damn whether I get anything to eat or drink or not, do you?" His voice was loud, getting louder. Two women at the next table turned around. They had been speaking Russian—probably they didn't know anything he said, only that he was angry at her. Lucy was embarrassed. "Please," she said. "Don't yell. It's only a pastry."

"But I told you. I told you I wanted something cold to drink and you order me this." His face was red. He held the coffee cup as though he meant to dash it in her face.

"I'm sorry," she said. "I tried." The women stared, talked to each other in low tones. Others in the shop glanced in their direction. Allen kept on, heaping every angry thing he could remember since they stepped off the plane.

All those women know is the tone of voice, Lucy thought. That he's upset. He could be screaming at me because I have a lover or I've overspent our checking account . . . a thousand things, and it's none of them. She was so tired. Her feet didn't ache now. They burned on the bottom. Felt scalded like the first sip of coffee on her tongue. She finished her torte, blew on her coffee. "How do they get it so hot?"

He glared at her, didn't answer. At least he was quiet. People in the shop had gone back to their own conversations, pastries. She felt like giggling. Did he know how ridiculous he had looked? Crazy Americans, they probably said, then shrugged their shoulders. Crazy.

Over the next few weeks, he repeated the insult of the coffee she'd gotten him when he had specifically asked her to get him a soda. She always let it drop. All she remembered was that he ruined a moment of small pleasure for her. That she had been both embarrassed and humiliated yet somehow able to step out of herself to see the humor in the whole damn thing.

Their last day in Denmark had been in the museum, his joy. He'd been bubbling before some of the paintings, excited, taking her hand like a child. "Come see this one. Marvelous craftsmanship. I'm overwhelmed." He could study a painting from twenty different angles, across the room, up close, over his shoulder. "Great composition. Look how he slants that light."

She looked at suits of armor, portraits of people who

looked starched and stuffed with straw. All the rooms were beige with beige carpeting, beige-cushioned benches in the center. Some were near windows. She sat on those occasionally, packed her suitcases in her mind.

"What's wrong with you?" he said. "Can't you concentrate?" He took her shoulders, turned her to face him. "Can't we do one thing *I*'m interested in?"

She didn't answer. They walked to the next room and he lost himself in another painting. "God, I wish I had my camera. The one museum in the world that allows you to use cameras and I don't have mine. Damn."

His camera was still broken. They had passed a dozen camera shops since it jammed and he refused to do in, let them look it over. "I'd have to explain it to them," he said. "They wouldn't know what I was talking about."

"You could point," she said. "It's amazing how much you can explain with a smile, gestures, and patience."

He didn't have the smile very often and he certainly didn't have the patience. She stopped suggesting camera shops, that he try to get it repaired.

She stopped sitting on benches in the rooms of the museum, instead stood before windows and looked across the green lawn circled with trees whose branches seemed to float. On the lawn families walked babies in strollers, boys threw Frisbees that were caught by other boys. People walked dogs. One couple sat in folding chairs, read. There was another wide lawn behind the museum. People picnicked with spread-out cloths, bottles of wine, long loaves of bread they broke and dipped into bowls. In the center of the lawn lay a woman on a blanket. She wore a straw hat tied under her chin with a purple scarf, sunglasses and sandals. Otherwise she was nude. Completely naked. She had narrow hips, long legs, and very large breasts. She too was reading and looked completely comfortable where she was, as she was. No one paid any attention to her.

Allen called from across the room, "This guy was a genius. I've never seen such brushwork."

She walked away from the window. "Yes," she said, "that is a good painting. I like the light."

He put his arm around her. "I want to go back to several paintings again. Really spend some time with them before we catch the train. Do you mind?"

"Of course not."

"You can stay here or go with me. There's a museum shop on the bottom floor, a place to have coffee."

"I'll get some cards," she said, and followed the arrows to the stairs. If she stayed here, he'd see the nude woman, destroy the beauty, naturalness of the whole scene. He'd stare. He'd talk about it later. "Of all the nudes we saw, all those people naked on the beach, not a one of them had anything worth showing. Worth looking at." They he'd say, "The best-looking one I saw was in downtown Copenhagen, broad daylight," laugh at his pun, describe the scene, embellish all of it. Destroy it for her.

Later when he talked on and on of the nude beaches, she smiled, said nothing.

A camera shop at the airport fixed his camera, didn't charge him anything. All he did was fuss about the good photos he missed, the great shots. He fussed in the tone of voice of a small child who stamps his foot, a very spoiled child.

Friends and Oranges

Michelle and I

TEEN ANGELS. WE lie to our mothers. We say we have to study. Algebra, history, awful biology. But she is a year older, Mother says, not in your class. She can help, I say. It is choir practice night. On Sundays we sing like angels. Our robes have wings. We lift and float over the rolling music to the pious sea. We like being almost bad. We like being so very, very good. Old ladies with saggy crepe arms pat our smooth and shiny heads. We wear thin dresses, tiny heels, straps of nothing shoes. When we sing, we arch our white throats sweet as song sparrows.

We have to practice, we have to study. We go to the movies. *Sadie Thompson* with Rita Hayworth, José Ferrer. A cat cries in the alley. She is thin and white with clear green eyes. We hold her, stroke her, say kitty, kitty things. We have to hurry, take the cat along. Mikki buys the tickets. I hide the cat inside my sweater. It does not cry out, but kneads my skin with soft, firm paws.

In the movie the cat sleeps, takes turns on our laps. Afterwards, Mikki and I walk home, carry the cat. We name the cat "Sadie"; discuss the movie. Why was it called *Rain*? Why are men so mean? Mikki doesn't answer. Sadie, who was so light, is now all heavy legs and fur.

We sleep at Mikki's house. Her mother has changed the sheets and the four-poster bed is a summer hill. Under the window, the mock orange blooms and thorns. Its fingers scratch the screen like a peeping tom. We open the window, reach out and pick the teasing oranges. My favorite smell in the whole world, says Mikki, tossing them up. That's all they're good for. Smell. She throws me one for under my pillow. It is mapped and green, fuzzy as a baby's head. The room is all citrus and flowers. We sleep in the top of a blossom tree, Mikki profile. Her nose and chin in the light are sharply drawn and beautiful. I prop on my elbow, watch her eyelids flutter as though she watches a movie. She moans and whimpers like a child; a three-year-old with bad dreams, half-asleep, afraid in the dark. I rub her hand and arms and finally sleep in the special scent of her.

Next morning, Sadie is gone. No one let her out, but she is nowhere we can find. Mikki and I look and call all the way to school, but the cat has disappeared.

Girl Graduates

I help Mikki pack. Plaids and sweaters, pajamas and socks, panties for each day of the week; Saturday embroidered in red, Sunday crude blue on shining yellow. We hug, promise to write. I do, Mikki doesn't. A year later, I pack and go away to school, meet a hundred girls, gossip and pry, pick and giggle. Mikki is a mugging photo, a silly two pages in my annual, something pressed like flowers between rough paper and leather bound.

Once, home for Christmas, someone calls. It's me, she shouts, it's Mikki. I'm at Mother's. We talk old times. Friends and boys, clothes and parents, school, books and friends. We promise to write. I do. She doesn't. In the summer I go to work for a dentist, wear a uniform crisp as paper, say Yes Doctor, Of Course Doctor, Certainly Doctor. I hand him tools, smile all the time, feel good and clean and tired, tired, tired. Mikki goes out West with a friend. She writes a card picture of the desert. You ought to see the colors. You would not believe how brilliant. I am sending you some. Look out.

My second year I marry. An artist. He is tall and thin and full of dreams. He smokes a lot, waves his hands when he talks, lives in museums and galleries. He paints, goes to school at night. I work in a department store. Lingerie. You would not believe the styles and patterns. Old ladies gasp. Teens giggle. I cook and clean and scrub his paints off furniture, shirts, the bathroom sink. Titian, Umber, Cadmium, Venetian. The words ring in my head. He is so full of Eakins, Homer, Whistler, Wyeth, and Wyeth. I am a study for a still life without apples.

He graduates, goes to work for an agency where the heads snap and roll. He is regarded as eccentric, a genius, highly creative, an exceptional individual. I am regarded as the artist's wife who makes babies and marvelous pies. I am a commercial for all the well-known brands. I know which are best and fast and better priced. I recite them like an alphabet, a spelling bee, and win. How clever. All my friends are into Tupperware and Sara Coventry. I listen well, learn that language. What you can store where, in what and for how long. Miracles of Tutankhamen's tomb. What you wear with jade and pearls.

Another Christmas

Michelle marries. Mother sends me a clipping from the

paper, *Central News and Views*. An announcement and paragraph of a shower her mother gave. Finger sandwiches, pastel mints, assorted nuts. There is nothing I can send Mikki but good wishes and a pot for tears. Who is Barton Francis Roberts III? Mikki's western friend? A few days after New Year's mother sends another clipping. Mikki on the front page of the *News and Views*. New Mother and Baby of the Year. Five hundred dollars in prizes. Mikki has a ribbon in her hair, a smile like Mona Lisa's sister. Her picture tells me nothing a stranger wouldn't know.

A year later, her mother sees my mother in the beauty shop. They each have standings. Mikki and Rob have moved to Texas. They are building a lovely home. Something on the order of Tara. They have horses, a pool.

They have another child. Someone sends me a clipping. Is it Mother? There is no note. The postmark is smeared.

My husband wins awards, frames and hangs them in the den. Soon he has the whole wall. He works nights, holidays, weekends. He is brilliant in design, grows a mustache, sings country/western in the shower.

What do you do, people ask at parties. I tell them I am an astronomer, a conchologist, a doctor, a lawyer, a princess, a tax collector and thief. They say how wonderfully talented you are. I do so many things well. My, we are a wonderful team. They haven't heard a word I said.

My husband plays the guitar, sings "The Wreck of the Edmund Fitzgerald." Everyone applauds. He hands me the case to carry. I bow. Thank you very much, I play better, but only at home.

In a class at the Y, I find a wheel, learn to spin. It takes me a year to center. I throw and throw, develop glazes, show my work. The rest of the time, I am my husband's wife, president of the PTA, carpool queen and Bear Cubs mother. Isn't this what you wanted, he says. All hours, wheels in my head turn the clay into forms.

One day Mikki calls. I'm here, she says. I'm in town. I'm

coming to see you. I give her directions. Past the Golden Arches, the Kentucky Fried, the Innerbelt, the cemetery, the brick breezeway and lighted lanterns and third box on the left. We laugh and laugh. She sounds the same. I'm into clay, I tell her. She screams, I'm into fibers. You ought to see my work. It's good. It's different. I think it will sell. I wait with the coffeepot and hot brownies, clean hands and house. Mikki never comes. Did I dream her voice? Fibers? I told you, my husband says. She's always been like that. Unpredictable. Unstable. What did you ever see in her? What kind of friend is she?

Down on the Farm

We buy some land, with house and barn, pastures, fences, sheep, cows, chickens and two large dogs. My husband wants to paint his greatest thing. He needs quiet. I take the children to school fifteen miles away, become the long-distance carpool queen, shop the six stores in town, buy little, have sodas in a bitter-smelling, marble-cool drugstore. I see myself in the mirror behind the counter. My face above the oranges, limes, bananas waiting to be used, my dark eyes. I ask if anyone is in there. One eye waters and cries.

The sheep die, cows break fences, eat corn, wander away. Pigs get big and hard to discipline. The barn falls, fences sprawl, drag their wire bellies. There is a drought and our crops burn, savings melt. We have great green thunderstorms with lightning that zips open the sky, rains hard balls of hail. The roof leaks and we sleep in ruin until a panel truck ruts up the rocky drive. The roofer is a naked man in boots. He has an even tan, only works in good weather. I like his voice, his wide shoulders, his quick and fun hands. He whistles down the chimney, adjusts the gutters, smooths the hearth.

My husband paints. He paints an apple, a chicken, and

finally a nude. Our neighbor poses. Her hair is long and blond and thin. It brushes her buttocks like a hand. She stands on a crop of far rocks in the pasture. My husband gets excited. Did you ever see such skin? The way the light reflects? He sits by the pond for water. I braid cattails by the creek, wade, pick wildflowers and watch. The work gets in a show and everyone asks did you pose? Of course, I answer. See my long blond hair, my lovely skin. He never asked. The artist's wife is always last. I am plain and brown, dusty as a wren. A mother mouse with her tail snapped in a trap.

Clay is all I know. I make flat things into something that holds and waits empty to hold again.

I Take a Saturday Off

The kiln is emptied and cool. My wheel wiped clean as an after-dinner platter. The pots sit in rows on shelves of hope. All day Catherine and I lie in a field of red clover. The air is all lavender and thick honey. I could eat it and fly. We count birds, began the count that morning with a pair of pileated woodpeckers. We write them down. Bluebirds, flickers, red-eyed vireos, kingbirds, doves. A red-tailed hawk. This is a dangerous sport, she says. Her binoculars are black and heavy against my chest. Field larks. She points, holds my eyes with her hand. Nine, she whispers. Last year we counted an even dozen in this spot. I watch the brown arrows dart and fan in the blue. I have never felt so happy. Alive in every humming cell. The top of my head feels electric. If I reached out my hand, touched Cath, we'd both be illuminated. She stands, reaches down for me. We have to go now, she says. We have hungry husbands and children waiting. I never want to go but take her cool hand that still smells of fresh water where we swam in the creek, of willow and wet fern.

Did you have fun, my husband asks? Tweet, tweet. He has

built a rock wall, piled stone upon stone upon stone. All the ones I liked best where they were. I knew them there. Now there are pock marks in the pasture, gaps in my daily walk. How dare he? How could he?

Someone had to stop the erosion, he shrugs. What is one wall against a mile? He is the Dutch boy with his finger in the dike. The whole damn wall.

Michelle Again

It's me, she calls, I'm coming out. This time she does. All in black, like a widow, mourning. She wears a sheer black dress with sweeping balloon sleeves; long black gloves, a large black braided hat. Her hair is up and hidden. Her face opaque as a cloud, and her eyes are gray and full of hurt. She is all silver and black and sad. I got the children, she says. That's all. Would you believe? His boss's wife. I believe. She hooks her arm around my husband's waist. Tell me, she coos, are all artists sexy? She bats her eyes, pale lashes and transparent lids. Would you want to paint me nude she asks? Want a mortgage, I seethe. I know where there's a big one. It goes with him.

After she leaves, he says she is not his type. Too clingy, too much heavy perfume. Magnolia, I say, tons of magnolia. Oh, Mikki, how could you?

In my potting shed, I turn and turn. The clay is me. Raku and sawdust, fire and water. I glaze and etch, sand and salt and fire. The kids complain. You never cook. I burn and bake with life. Sometimes when I tuck them in, my hands are dry and rough. There is mud under my nails. They don't like the smell. It is all I have. I am the clay.

Mikki Comes Again

She is different this time. She is copper and red. Her nose

is tipped, her smile recapped, she has diamonds in her eyes, on her hands, at her throat. William is in stocks. She met William at a Parents Without Partners meeting. Only William isn't a parent. Don't tell anyone, she cautions. He came to meet people and guess who he found? Tra-la . . . little ole me, she sings. Across the smoky room. William is so rich. He buys me everything. A condo, a car . . . a white MG. We're learning to fly, she says. Now he wants a plane.

What about your weaving, I ask. Who has time? She blows smoke at the ceiling. It is so dusty and full of lint and lonely. She wants a farm like ours. All the joys and charm of country life. But William won't live on a farm she says. Not in a thousand years, he only needs the write-off. You got the bright idea, my husband says.

The farm they buy is in the next county. Mikki says it has sixty cows, but not the milking kind. How do you know? William asks. He looks deep into her eyes. Mikki can't believe him. Isn't he cute? She says he is a prince. A man in his prime. He writes poetry. Brings her a poem a day with a vitamin like a rose. She can't believe he is real. He is everything she always wanted. Everything. She does not look at me when she says this. After she leaves, I look around. The poor farm, my husband with his paints, my filled potting shed . . . and God knows the kids. Who is kidding whom?

I Go on the Road with a Green Chair

The beanbag chair wears my husband's hat. Dumb, he says. But I am afraid to travel three hundred miles alone. I need a male companion. The green chair beside me has a thick neck, wears a pulled-down black felt hat. Little old man. Quiet fellow. I leave at 5:00 a.m. in the dark. A van chases me fifty miles through dense forest. All my doors are locked, the gas tank full, no one else on the road. I speed, hope for a ticket, listen for sirens, finally lose the van. The

beanbag chair slumps to the dash. I stop in a city for breakfast, cut my hand on a map, leave bloody prints, a trail for
whoever has to look when I am kidnapped, raped, and killed.
All day I sell my work. I can't price and wrap pots fast
enough. That night I stay with friends. You work too hard,
they say. Come have fun with us. I call home. Are you
painting, I ask? It's too quiet, he says, come home. At the
end of the week, I limp ragged home, rip off my ERA for
Everyone sticker, and fall in the door. He wants to have fun,
go out to eat and dance, drink wine, make love. I want to
sleep and sleep and sleep. At least a hundred years. At least
until the true prince wakes me up and someone has cleaned
out the kingdom. The Agean world of the house.

My husband has learned to cook. He can read packages,
measure, time, and taste. He can wash and dry, but not fold
or find homes for the mingled crowd of clothes that hovers
in the laundry room door. He has watered my plants and
each one greets me like a favorite child.

The children have gone to live with friends. They never
plan to return. They are sixteen and mature. Who needs
adults? They have jobs, cars, school, friends. They have tennis and music, disco and pinball.

In my pottery shed, I throw mud against the world that
never stops. It turns like time, a spinning clock that wears
my face.

My husband's work does not sell. He says no one knows
what great art really is. He refuses to paint birds or flowers,
wildlife or friends. He hates buckets and wagons, old barns,
wants to paint his message to the world, repent at leisure.

A piece of my pottery is accepted in a museum show.
Porcelain pears in a lattice basket. They display it under
glass. My husband asks, are you proud of that? That? Yes.
It's an original. It's beautiful and I made it. He walks away.
Ha. A museum guard stares. Are you the artist? Yes, I answer. The word seeks my husband, finds and taps him on
the shoulder. He turns around. Come on, he says, let's get
out of here.

He paints a weathered board with rusty nails and insect writing. It looks real, I tell him, really nice, really good. Behind the wood and through a hole, he paints his eye. A blue vision. Do you realize that is your eye? It is your self-portrait. Call it *Self-Portait of the Artist as an I*. He makes an ugly noise in his nose. I make a pot with the same name and nose, mustache and glasses. It sells to a collector and I pay the current bills. My husband never asks when the money comes, where it goes. Bills come to stay like aged relatives, grow cantankerous and ill, but never die.

He has another show. I help him pack and price and hang. I play good hostess with the cups of punch and good cheer. I circulate at the opening event. Isn't he great, people ask and reach for another glass. I know you are so proud. They say all the right things, but don't buy his work. One day he takes his books, mustache cup, guitar, and leaves. At first I hear strange noises. The house seems large and I am Alice who drank the wrong bottle. Then I learn to play the radio loud, dance by myself in all the places I never knew before.

Once Again the Cat

Mikki calls. I'm here, she yells. It's me. It's Mikki. I'll be out to see you. She drives a small red car, the dogs wag and lick the sweet air around her. She is slender gold and silver. She brings mock oranges in a basket. Aren't they marvelous? She holds one to her nose, juggles others in her arms. There's nothing like them in the world. She heaps them high in my largest blue pottery bowl. The room is alive with citrus smell.

Remember the cat? Mikki says. Sadie the cat? I thought you died. I hug Mikki. Her bones are sharp as saws and she feels light as knitting. I did, she laughs, O God, I did. I died. She says she has been through hell and home. William left. His secretary,—she rolls her green eyes. That old cliché. I should have known. The least suspected. Five psychiatrists pulled me through.

Why didn't you call? I ask. I couldn't talk, she says. All I did was cry. Not Mikki. I'm glad she didn't call. I wouldn't want to know, to see, to hear. Not Mikki.

But I won, she says. I won. You should have seen me on the stand. I was the perfect little wounded wife. The cast-aside waif. The judge held my hand, cheered me up. O that judge was great. And I got the condo, the car, five thou a month for the rest of my life . . . and—she screams—I got the farm. All that grass and crazy cows and house and barn are mine. He fought like a fish, a big, big fish, but I won.

I pour red wine into new goblets still warm from the kiln. Their glaze is smooth as Mikki's skin. We finish the bottle and another, talk silly, then serious. We compare battle scars, wounds from war. Mikki lost her breasts, I my uterus. The crocheted scar is pink from my crotch to my waist. What a waste, we lament and laugh. Then march like veterans in a no day parade. Mikki, I open my arms, welcome home. Her eyes are the same. Sadie the cat. O Sadie the cat.